CLAIMING
Mine

Zara

#AlwaysLast

Prologue

Ana

HAVE YOU EVER HAD THE FEELING YOU WERE BEING WATCHED? EVER felt the tiny hairs on the back of your neck stand on end and shivers run down your spine, only to turn and find no one there?

I get that feeling, but he *is* there. I know better than to let him get to me, but he does. *Every time.*

He smiles at me and takes a drink of his coffee, and my body heats from his intense gaze.

Ace McGowan.

Aka Sergeant-at-Arms for the Unforgiven Riders.

I couldn't escape him if I wanted to.

You see, I work for his mum, in her café: Nancy's Coffee Nook. I have for the past twelve months.

I shake my head and walk over to the table recently vacated by an elderly couple, where I stack the dirty plates and struggle to pick up the two mugs as well. I turn back to walk towards the kitchen, when the plates start to topple. In a flash, Ace is there, saving the day.

"I got them, babe." His deep, husky voice resonates through my body. He always has the power to make my lady parts tingle— and he knows it.

"Thank you," I whisper.

"No problem, baby." I shiver when he calls me 'baby' or 'babe'. Most women don't like the endearment, thinking a bloke only uses it because he doesn't remember the girl's name, but when Ace says it to me, it does things to my body. I try to hide the effects, but I fail every, single time.

"Can I get you anything else?" I ask, knowing he always has one of my homemade, mini heart-shaped chocolate cakes. They're a simple chocolate sponge, with a raspberry cream filling and covered in chocolate ganache.

"You know what I want," he states, his gravelly voice causing goose bumps to appear over my skin. *Oh Bugger.*

His smirk says it all: he saw the effect he has on me. I close my eyes and take a deep breath. This back and forth has been going on for over a year—ever since Nancy, Ace's mum, gave me a job here in her café after I rolled into town.

A shiver of a different kind—a nasty kind—snakes down my spine as I remember why I fled to this town with my sister. My past surges up to greet me, bringing with it all the pain he caused. But I push it back, refusing to let it darken my new life and praying it never catches up with me.

Leaving was the safer option for me.

I open my eyes and look straight at the man who owns my heart—and who has the power to tear that heart into a million pieces. His eyes are a pale green and stand out against his tanned skin and the well-trimmed beard he's sporting. His dark hair is shaved at the sides and back, the length on top slightly slicked back, but not in a way that says he uses gel or hair products. More like he's pushed it back with his hand, running his fingers through it all the time.

"I can't be what you want, Ace," I whisper.

It's like being on a merry-go-round with him.

"Yes, you can; you just don't know it. Go out with me, Ana." He picks up a piece of my hair and rubs it between his fingers. Our gazes are locked in some kind of tug of war with each other, neither one of us wanting to break the connection. But gradually, my head forces my eyes away.

"I can't." I take a step back, hoping he will leave the subject alone.

I can see the annoyance on his face. I seem to piss him off whenever he tries this, but I need to stick to my guns. I can't be hurt again, and I know Ace can hurt me—not physically, but hurt me nonetheless.

"We'll see." He leaves me standing there and heads for the door without a backwards glance. I watch his back as chairs start to scrape across the floor. I feel the first touch of lips on my cheek and can't stop myself from smiling.

The boys from the MC kiss me on the cheek, one by one, adding their thanks for the breakfast and coffee. First Batch, then EC, then Pitch, and finally Dyson. I have to look up to smile at the boys because they are all well over six feet tall—plus, it doesn't take much to be taller than me.

Dyson winks at me and whispers, "Wait for it, Mouse." He steps away, after using my nickname the boys in the MC have given me.

I frown at him, just before I see Ace marching back towards us. My breath catches in my throat as he gets closer and closer. He comes to a complete stop in front of me and cradles my jaw in such a soft touch I have to blink a few times just to make sure it's really Ace.

"Always last." He kisses my cheek, over the exact place where the boys just laid their 'thank you' kisses. The kiss is so sweet that I get lost in the soft touch, his scent invading my senses—Ace always wears Paco Rabanne aftershave. Our eyes lock before he turns and walks out of the cafe, leaving me gaping like a fish out of water. Damn that man for making me feel like this. He's making me want more. More with him.

More with Ace McGowan could be the best thing for me, or he could ruin me for all men who follow.

One

Ana

I WIPE THE TEARS FROM UNDER MY EYES AND TRY TO CONTROL MY breathing. Nancy just broke the news that her cancer is back, and by back, I mean with a freaking vengeance. She has a few weeks to live. The cancer has spread throughout her body. She has known for some time but didn't want to bother anyone with the news. She knew there wasn't anything that could be done.

#FuckCancer

I hate that she's having to go through this again. I wasn't around the first time she had it, but she's told me the stories. Nancy has breast cancer and it's spread to her bones. She kept her illness a secret for a long time, knowing it had progressed to the point there was no cure, and is now refusing any form of treatment.

Ace is angry; he's yelling and bossing people around, snapping at anyone who comes within breathing distance of him. The boys help with calming him down, but sometimes he needs to vent.

I can hear him shouting at someone in the café, and I stay hidden in the back of the kitchen, trying to compose myself. I hate seeing Ace like this. He's normally so strong, but I can see he is devastated by the news that his mum only has a few weeks to live.

"I don't fucking care if your tea is luke-fucking-warm. Fuck off to another cafe if you don't like it," he screams, and I can only assume a customer has made him react like this.

I take a deep breath and walk out the front to try and calm him down.

He's standing over a man around my age, who is shaking in his chair. I hope he doesn't pee himself. I don't fancy clearing that, and I can't see Ace McGowan cleaning up urine.

"Ace." I stomp over to him and he snaps his head in my direction. His narrowed eyes don't scare me. Nothing about him scares me—other than when he's trying to get into my knickers, and my heart.

"Leave the man alone," I state, putting my hands on my hips. Ace cocks an eyebrow at me but I don't allow any emotion other than annoyance show.

"Fuck that! He was bitching because his tea isn't hot enough."

"Ace, it's fine. We'll get him another cup, it's not a problem."

"Bullshit. He can take his shitty comments elsewhere. You are rushed off your feet, so lukewarm tea is the least of your fucking problems." I sigh and lay a hand on his forearm. The heat from his skin sears my hand. I don't normally touch him, from fear of my body reacting to his.

This touch just proves my point.

My being tingles at the contact and my breathing picks up. Ace straightens his back at the minor changes in my body. The anger slips away and a smirk slides into place.

Bugger.

Ace looks down at my hand on his arm and then back up to my face, where our eyes connect. I pull away like his skin burned me and tuck my hands into the pockets of my maxi skirt, shifting my gaze around the room. Some people are staring at us, but others are just getting on with their day. I think our regulars are used to the MC boys being in here.

"Always better," Ace says. Dyson sniggers from behind him but Ace keeps his eyes locked on me. My gaze snaps to Dyson and he winks at me.

"What?" I ask, but think better of it. "Do you know what? Never mind. Sir, I will get you a new cup of tea, on the house of course."

"The fuck you will." Ace's voice booms through the room. People gasp from his outburst but I just stare at him.

"Ace McGowan, I suggest you stop this instant." Nancy's voice comes from behind the counter. I didn't even see her come in. She's lost quite a bit of weight and her appetite is almost non-existent. She winces a little before my sister, Zarah, helps her to a nearby chair. Ace moves swiftly to be by his mother's side. My heart swells at seeing this bad-arse biker man go all soft like a marshmallow over his ill mother.

"I think you should leave," Batch says to the man complaining about his tea. He nods nervously and pretty much runs from the cafe. The rest of the MC brothers chuckle at the man bolting.

"Pussy," EC mutters. I give him a stern look and he shuts up. These boys act all tough and hard, but when a woman they respect gives them the eyes and a stern talking to, they crumble. These boys respect me, and on some level I think that's down to Ace and Nancy. But I also think these boys know how to treat women. Yeah, they sleep around, but they never give the girls false hope that they will get more out of their session with them.

"Don't you lot have somewhere else to be?" I ask the table.

"Nah, Mouse," EC replies with a cheeky grin. EC aka Eye Candy is the pretty boy of the club. He only has to smile, and the ladies drop their knickers. Shameless.

"We're on a break, pretty girl. We work hard as fuck, ya know," Batch pipes in. I laugh and walk closer to the table.

"You—work hard? Are you joking?"

"Nah, babe."

"Batch," Ace growls from behind me. I turn to see him still kneeling in front of Nancy, but his gaze firmly locked on Batch.

"Yeah, yeah. I know, fucker." My eyes snap back to Batch and he shrugs at me.

"Do you know what? I don't wanna know." I walk over to the table the man just vacated and start to clear away the dirty cups and plates. I stack them up and make my way out the back to the kitchen. Once I'm there I load up the dishwasher and see how Zarah is doing with the lunch orders.

"You okay?" I ask her. She lifts her head up and smiles at me.

"Yeah, just need to add the gravy to this and you can take the food out. You okay?"

"I'm okay." I know my voice doesn't convince her. She frowns at me and I sigh. "Ace again."

"When are you going to let yourself be happy again, Ana? Not all men are like the knobhead. Ace could be good for you," she states. I know she only wants what's best for me but letting go and being with Ace could ruin me. I inhale a deep breath and take the two plates of roast chicken out to the customers.

I look around the room, a little disappointed to see the boys are gone. My heart sinks at the thought that Ace left without saying goodbye. God, this man has my mind in a tizzy. I see Nancy is still sitting in her chair, chatting to a lady next to her. I smile and walk over to them.

"Do you need anything, Nance?" She looks up at me and offers a smile, a smile that could light up the bloody world. Nancy is not afraid of dying; she has made that perfectly clear. She sat me down yesterday and told me she wanted to live her life in the cafe and around her family rather than vomiting in the bathroom for her remaining days. I cried myself to sleep that night, with Zarah holding me tightly.

"I'm good, my darling. Ace said he would see you tonight." She winks at me. She's made it known that she wants us to be together, but I keep shooting her idea down. She knows about Gary—I broke down not long after me and Zarah arrived here and she took us in—and she is adamant Ace and the boys can protect me, but I don't want to bring my troubles to the club. We have gone over and over this time and time again.

"I'm not going, Nance. I have told him this and I'm sticking to my decision. I don't belong there. I've seen the women who hang around, and I don't fit in. I don't *want* to fit in. Ace needs to understand that."

"But, Ana—" I cut her off.

"No. I need to do this for me." I walk away before I upset her. I know she wants her son to be happy, but I can't give that to him. I can't bring him into my troubles. I refuse to. She's told me Ace and the club will help, but this is my problem, not theirs.

The rest of the day goes without any other issues. A guy comes in and flirts with Zarah, and she takes him up on going out for a drink later tonight. It's nice to see her living her life. Maybe one day I will too; just not now.

We close the cafe and make our way home, Zarah talking about her date tonight all the way. She talks about what she's going to wear, even though they're only going to a pub in town, and I listen to her and think about when I first started dating Gary. He was great in the beginning, but we had a rush wedding because I fell pregnant. He wanted us married before the baby came; told me his kid wouldn't be known as a bastard.

Not long after we married, I lost the baby. I was thirteen weeks pregnant at the time and it devastated me. Gary changed after that. He became abusive, both physically and mentally. He controlled every part of my life until I had no friends or family. I was only twenty at the time. I lost my parents not long after that, so my world became a very dark place to me.

Zarah was the only shining light in my life because she refused to leave me alone. She would make a point of bumping into me when I was actually allowed out of the house.

Mine and Zarah's house is in a small cul-de-sac of new builds. We share the mortgage and all the other bills. It's great living with her.

"I'm going to have a quick shower and get ready. Dan is picking me up in an hour."

"Go. Get. Make yourself look pretty for this bloke." We're a strange dynamic, me and my sister. Zarah is thirty, two years older than me, but I'm wiser. I always acted like the older sister, until shit hit the fan with Gary. Zarah was always the wild child of the family.

I climb the stairs and walk into my room, stripping off my work clothes. Opening my drawer, I pull out my comfy cotton shorts and a tank top. Then I brush my hair out and tie it up in a messy bun. After throwing my dirty clothes into the washing basket, I head down to the kitchen to make myself a cup of tea.

I take my mug over to the patio doors that lead out to our very well-manicured garden, thanks to the MC boys. There is a flower bed along one side, filled with a variety of flowers—I like colours. The large tree at the bottom of the garden allows for perfect shade in the summer.

I never would have thought a bunch of bikers could clean up a garden and make it look pretty. They even added some solar fairy lights along the walls and some solar lights mixed in with the flowers.

I sit on the white bench Zarah found at a car boot sale one Sunday and take in the evening weather. The sun is still high in the sky. It's summer here in England, so we get sunlight until around nine p.m. We enjoy the nice weather whenever we have it because it could be raining tomorrow. Luckily, we're supposed to have sunny weather all week.

I lose track of time while reading a sexy rock-star book. Who doesn't love rock-star triplets? A knock at the front door startles me from my reading bubble. I slap my hand over my heart and calm my rapid breathing. After placing my Kindle down on the bench, I walk through the house to the front door, giving a quick glance at the clock on the wall and noticing it's just before eight-thirty.

I pull the door open, not expecting who is on the other side.

"What are you doing here?" I ask my visitor.

"Why, were you expecting some other bloke to visit you at this time of night?" I shake my head at him.

"I'm here alone, Ace. Zarah is out on a date with some guy she met today at the cafe. But again: what are you doing here?" He folds his arms across his chest, making the black t-shirt tighten around his biceps. His club cut fits him like a glove. So does the sexy leather jacket he wears during the winter months. His green eyes shine bright under the security light, and they bore into mine as I wait for an answer to my question.

"You didn't come to the club party. Why?" I sigh and wrap my arms around my middle, protecting myself from this man.

"You know why, Ace. When are you going to understand that we," I wave my hand between us, "can't happen." He sighs and drops his hands before inching forward and resting his forearms on the doorframe, leaning into the house just a little. My heart skips a beat at how close he is. This is what Ace McGowan does to me. He affects me so bloody much. The little touches that have passed between us over the past year have made it almost unbearable to be around him.

"Why? Clearly you find me attractive, and you know I find you sexy as fuck. So why?"

"No," I state.

"Why?" he asks again. I sigh.

"Because I said so, Ace."

"Not good enough. We could be so fucking good together." He winks at me. My heart is racing like a stampede in the jungle.

"Because, I..." I stop myself. I suck in a sharp breath and my eyes snap to his. His eyes narrow and he tilts his head, taking in my words and my worried facial expression.

"Because, what, Ana? And do not think of lying to me." I can see he's getting pissed. His fists are now at his sides and clenching repeatedly. He takes a deep breath and goes to open his mouth to speak, but a car door slamming has him spinning around and covering me.

God, this man. He protects me without hesitation.

I look over his shoulder and see a police car, then I notice two officers coming towards me. My breath catches in my throat. Oh no—Zarah. I step closer to Ace, and he wraps his arm around my waist.

"Miss Ana Dawkins?" the male officer asks. I nod but don't speak. Ace talks for me.

"What can we do for you, officers?" They both look between Ace and me, and the female officer is probably thinking why he is with a plain-looking woman like me. Ace pulls me tighter when he sees the female officer sizing him up.

"We have a Zarah Dawkins in the emergency department at hospital. She was attacked but she isn't talking. She only speaks when she asks for you. We got your information from her hospital records."

"Oh, my G—" A sob breaks from me and my knees feel weak. Ace holds me to him, supporting my body.

"I'll make sure she gets to the hospital safely." Ace's voice comes from above me. I wrap my arms around his body and take some of his strength, before facing the officers.

"How badly hurt is she?" I manage to ask.

The female officer answers. "She was badly beaten. We are unsure of the full extent of her injuries. The doctors will explain better when you get there." I nod and pull away from Ace. I need to get changed and grab an overnight bag for my big sister.

"Did you catch the fucker who did it?" Ace's voice is tense. My gaze snaps back to the three people standing at my door as I wait for the officers' answer, and going by the look on their faces, I'm not going to like it.

"No, we didn't."

Ace

I TAKE MY PHONE OUT OF MY POCKET AND SEND DYSON A QUICK text. He's the club's VP, and the son of our club president, Suede. He needs to know what's happening. We're a clean club, but we can also be a mean bunch of bastards when we need to be.

And we don't take too kindly to fuckers beating on women and kids.

Dyson responds, telling me he will meet us at the hospital. I stand by the door, waiting for my woman to emerge from her room.

Yeah, Ana is my woman, even if she doesn't see it yet, or want it.

She will.

I know she's hiding some shit from me, and I will find out what it is. Her sister, Zarah, knows what it is; I can see it in the way she so desperately wants Ana to be happy. Zarah has often tried to get Ana to give me a chance, and I'm grateful for it because I believe I can give her what she wants.

Yeah, I may sound like a cocky cunt, but who the fuck cares. I can have any woman I want, but I want Ana Dawkins.

A noise from down the hall has me turning to see Ana walking towards me with an overnight bag in her tiny hand. She's changed into blue jeans that fit her legs perfectly, and a red sweatshirt with a white heart on it. She's slipped her feet into a pair of trainers.

As she gets closer to me and I take the overnight bag from her, I watch as she slips her handbag over her head. She picks up her phone and looks for her house keys, but I have them.

"I have them, babe. Come on, let's go and see your sister, yeah?" She nods silently, and my heart hurts for her. Zarah is not only her sister but her best friend also. They are extremely close.

I walk her out to my bike and hand her the helmet, but she doesn't take it.

"You need to put a helmet on if you're riding with me, baby."

"Then I won't go with you. I'll take my car. I can't ride that, Ace," she states. Yeah, that shit's not going to fly. She's riding at my back. End of conversation.

"I'm taking you to see your sister, so get on the bike. You're upset and you shouldn't be driving. Now is not the time to be a brat."

Wrong fucking thing to say. *Oh, fuck.* The look on her face tells me I should have stopped fucking talking.

"Seriously?" Her hands rest on her hips and I can't help but chuckle. Her frown deepens but I leave her standing there and sling my leg over my bike.

"Yeah, I'm serious. Get on the bike."

"Ace, I—"

"Get on the fucking bike, Ana." She snatches the helmet from my hand and tugs it on her head, before strapping it in place. She looks at the seat, then back to me.

"What?" I snap.

"How do I get on? I told you I've never been on a motorcycle before." I shake my head at her, but I know I shouldn't because she's never been in the MC life. I need to set things straight with her.

Since learning of my mum's terminal illness, I've been

viewing the world differently, understanding just how short life truly is. The things you love can be taken from you in a split second, so like fuck am I going to allow Ana to continue believing nothing is going to happen between us.

"Place your hand on my shoulder and throw your leg over the bike. Put both feet on the pegs." I point to the pegs and then the exhaust pipe. "And don't touch that pipe, it gets fucking hot and I don't want anything to happen to those sexy legs of yours." I wink at her and she blushes.

There's my shy girl.

Ana listens to my instructions and climbs on behind me. She's unsure of where to put her hands, so she gingerly rests them on my hips.

Yeah, not happening, baby. Around the waist they go.

I grip her hands and pull them around my waist, settling them on my lower abdomen. I bet she's blushing up a storm behind me. My cock swells in my jeans at the thought of her pale skin, darkening to a sultry rose, and juicy when I get a hold of it. And that arse of hers... fuck me; my handprint will look sexy against her pale cheeks.

I start the bike and rev the engine. My girl's arms tighten around me and my cock takes notice of how close she really is. The fucker is sick and tired of being blue, but unless it's Ana giving him relief, I'm not interested. Hell, I haven't even fucked a club girl in nearly a year.

I pull away from her house and make my way towards the hospital, which only takes nearly thirty-minutes. I spot where my boys are parked and pull alongside them. I kill the engine and climb off the bike, before turning to help Ana off. I wait until she's solid on her feet before I pull the overnight bag out of my saddlebags.

"Let's go," I say, taking her hand and pulling her towards the boys and the hospital door. Each of the boys nod and smiles at

Ana. They are protective of her, just as much as I am, even though I haven't officially claimed her as my old lady.

We make it through the emergency department and the nurse tells us Zarah has been moved up to a room for the night. People move out of our way when we step off the lift at the ward where Zarah is being kept—people are always shit scared of us. They always seem to give us looks and a wide berth around town.

"Zarah Dawkins' room, please?" I ask the nurse at the nurses' station. She jumps at the sound of my voice, and her gaze snaps to mine before scanning the rest of the boys. Dyson, EC and Batch are here with me.

"Ummm, I don't. I ummm…" she stammers.

"Take a breath, sweetheart. Look at the computer and tell me what room Zarah Dawkins is in. Can you do that for me, darlin'?" EC's voice is calming with a hint of flirtation. The pretty-boy bastard can charm his way into anything and anyone—and I mean anything and anyone; men included.

EC is short for Eye Candy. He was given that name when he was a prospect because he flirted with a female cop and got us off a minor drug charge. He got to get his dick wet a few times with her too. He's a jammy bastard.

"She is in room twenty-four," she manages to say. Ana is still at my side, our hands locked together. I nod and leave EC chatting to the nurse. The boys are hot on my heels as we find Zarah's room.

"You okay?" I ask my girl when she hesitates at the door. She nods.

"I'm just scared of how she will look. She's my big sister, Ace. I know she's supposed to look out for me, but I look out for her, too. I feel like I let her down. I should have sensed something was off with that guy earlier." She looks down at the floor and my heart breaks a little for her. I use my forefinger to lift her chin, and bend my knees so we're eye to eye.

"None of this was your fault. None of this was Zarah's fault. The club will handle this. You got me?"

"No, Ace, you can—" I don't let her finish. I pinch her lips together, halting her words.

"I can and I fucking will. No one fucks with what is mine."

"But we aren't yours, Ace!" Ana steps away from me and opens the door, not even taking a breath before walking inside to see her sister. Fuck my life, when is she going to get it?

"Ace, you need to lock her down, brother. She's getting bolder with you, which means now is the perfect time to claim her." Dyson claps me on the back and walks into the room, Batch close behind.

I follow the boys and see Ana lying in the bed next to a very battered and beaten Zarah. The anger coming from the lads is palpable. I can see the need for blood in their eyes.

They hate seeing Zarah like this. Hell, they hate seeing my Ana hurting. Each of the boys step forward, one by one, and kiss Zarah's forehead. They would normally kiss her cheeks, but they are bruised to shit.

"Who did this, Z?" Batch asks her. She looks from Batch to Ana, and I wait for her to tell Batch to get lost, but she surprises me when she nods at her sister.

"His name is Dan Cook. He works down at the DIY store next to the shopping centre." Her voices cracks, and Ana pulls her closer, wanting to console her sister but trying not to hurt her at the same time.

"What are your injuries?" Dyson asks her gently. She takes a deep breath and explains.

"My face—obviously. He told me it was my face that got me in trouble with him, because I smiled at some random guy who held the door open for me at the pub. I also have two cracked ribs and the rest is only bruising. That's it." She cuddles into Ana more, as if she's her safety blanket.

"The club is handling this, okay?" Dyson grinds out, the anger evident in his voice. He leaves no room for questions. The club will take care of this prick.

"Okay. Do what you have to do," Zarah whispers.

"*Zarah!*" Ana yells. She rears back and glares at her older sister.

"I'm sorry, Ana, but Dan hurt me. He told me that a slut like me always gets what she wants by opening her legs and smiling at a guy. That is why he beat me. Since when is a beautiful woman to be blamed for being herself? I am beautiful—well, I was anyway."

"Still are beautiful," I snap.

"Maybe, Ace, but thank you. No woman should be made to feel like a slut because she smiles at people to be polite, or for being beautiful."

"That is not what I mean. The police will handle this, Zarah. The club doesn't need to get involved."

"They're already involved, Smallie." I've heard Z call Ana that nickname before at the café. It must be a childhood name.

"How, though?" Ana asks. Even her sister can see where things are going to go with us; I just wish Ana could see it. But she will see soon enough. I'm sick of this chasing shit that has been going on between us. No fucking more.

Zarah looks between Ana and me, and the boys chuckle. But when Ana snaps her gaze to them, they cough in an attempt to cover it up. Yeah, they know she has a mean streak when she needs to show it.

The doctor walks in, and to say she's a little shocked to see us is an understatement. Batch chuckles at her facial expression, the red blush giving her away. Her gaze snaps to his and her blush deepens.

Yeah, honey, you're not the only woman who blushes around my brother.

I turn my eyes back to my girl and her sister. Ana is climbing off the bed, so I step up beside her and wrap my arm around her waist, letting my hand settle on her hip.

"How are you feeling, Miss. Dawkins?" the doctor asks Zarah.

"I'm sore but I'll live. When can I go home?" she asks. The doctor flicks through her chart and then looks at Zarah.

"I would like to keep you in overnight at least. You took quite a beating. I really hope the police catch the bastard who did this to you. He needs a beating of his own." The boys nod and Batch speaks up.

"Oh, he will." The doc, to our surprise, just nods in understanding.

The Unforgiven Riders are known to the area and beyond, and not only in a good sense. We've had to throw our weight around a few times, but only when it was needed. Most of the older generation don't like us because we own a few businesses around here they don't fully approve of, but hey, we have to earn a living.

"Get some rest, Zarah," the doc states, and leaves the room, but not before casting one last look at Batch. Batch winks at her and she almost walks into the doorframe. The boys chuckle, and so does Zarah.

"Zarah, EC will stay the night with you, for protection. I don't think the fucknut will try and get to you again but I wanna be safe," Dyson explains to her. I nod my head, but Ana is shaking hers.

"I'm staying, Dyson. We'll be fine," Ana pipes in. *Yeah, not gonna happen.* She's staying in my bed tonight, or I'm staying in hers. I need to keep her close, because this bloke might try and get to her since he knows where they live.

"It's done, babe. EC stays." I growl when he calls her 'babe'. Ana looks at me and I nod.

"It has to be done, babe. You're coming home with me tonight.

I can protect you better at mine," I tell her, leaving no room for arguments.

"But—"

"Enough. It's decided, Ana. Can you trust me on this?" My voice is gentle but firm. I don't want her to be pissed at me.

She thinks it over but then nods, looking up at me with her sad, innocent eyes. It makes me want to lean in and kiss her, so that is what I do.

I rest my lips on hers, and her sharp intake of breath lets me slip my tongue into her warm mouth, as I slide my hands down her sides and let them rest on her hips, holding her firmly to me. One hand slips down to cup her firm arse all on its own —honestly.

I kiss my girl until we are both breathless.

Ana breaks our connection and steps back. She brings her fingers to her mouth, then bits her bottom lip

She shakes her head at me, letting me know she doesn't want to kiss me again, but I don't fucking care. That *will* be happening again, because kissing her has my cock hard as steel in my jeans.

"Ace. We can't—I've told you this before. Oh, God." Zarah touches her hand and Ana leans close to her and whispers something in her ear. Ana's eyes zone in on Zarah, and she nods. I frown at the sisters as they continue to talk, so quiet no one else in the room can hear them.

"Let's go," Ana whispers, her shoulders slumped. I can only imagine Zarah has told her to go with me for her own protection, and also for Zarah's peace of mind.

I nod to the boys and walk towards the door, following Ana.

"Keep me posted, yeah?" I say to Dyson. He nods.

Each of the boys lean in and kiss Ana's cheek, one by one. I clench my fists, but I see the boys' cheeky winks at her. They know what they're doing. I step up to Ana and place my hand on the small of her back, forcing her out of the room.

We take the lift in complete silence, followed by walking to my bike with no words shared. I go to hand her the helmet, but stop, instead bending forward and kissing her cheek, right over the spot where the boys kissed her.

"Always last," I say, before placing the helmet on her head and climbing onto my bike.

Three

Ana

Always last.

That's what Ace always says after the boys kiss my cheek. I have no clue why. He's so bloody *alpha male* about things. I bet he's like that with all the women he sleeps with.

My body shudders and my stomach revolts against the piece of toast I'm forcing down into my empty stomach. I'm standing in his kitchen, waiting for him to get off the phone with Suede, the President of the Unforgiven Riders.

My worry for Zarah is knotting my stomach. I hate that this happened to her. We are more than sisters; we are best friends. So when she hurts, I hurt.

I sip from my cup of hot tea and lean against the counter, appreciating the black marble worktop. I was surprised when Ace brought me here. I thought he was going to go to the clubhouse, where most of the men live these days. Ace's semi-detached house is next door to Batch's home.

I walk over to the patio doors that lead out onto a very manicured garden. There aren't many flowers like my own, but there are solar lights and two picnic benches, and a very large barbeque in the corner. The garden is big and connects the two houses together to make one massive garden.

Before he took the phone call, Ace was explaining the house and garden situation. He and Batch wanted a big garden for when they settled down, so their kids could play together, and they could have large family barbecues away from the club.

I feel arms wrap around my waist and tense up. I know Ace would never hurt me physically, but I can't stop my body from reacting.

"I would never hurt you; you know that. So why the tensing?" he asks, his warm breath on my ear.

"I know you wouldn't. But we can't happen, Ace." I pull away from him and he lets me. The frown on his face shouldn't be there. He's too handsome to be frowning.

Our eyes are locked in a war of want and need, but my walls refuse to come down just yet. My heart's not sure it can take any more pain caused by a man.

He sighs and walks over to the couch, where he sits down and kicks his feet up on the coffee table before switching the TV on. He leaves me standing there, with my thoughts running around my head.

It's Zarah's fault I'm here. She begged me to stay with him, said she would sleep better tonight if she knew I was safe. And she knew I would be safe with Ace. I take a deep breath and sit on the other side of the sofa from Ace. He's watching some cooking programme on Netflix, something about not being able to cook.

We don't speak.

He laughs a few times and my head keeps snapping in his direction, because when Ace smiles or laughs, it brightens up his entire face.

The show finishes and I look down at my phone clutched in my hand, checking the time. It's just past midnight. I yawn and climb to my feet. I bite my lip because I know what I have to ask, and I'm not sure I want to hear the answer.

"Umm, Ace, I'm kind of tired and want to go bed. Which room am I in?" The TV flicks off and Ace stands. He turns and walks towards the stairs, without a word to me. I close my eyes and will the stupid tears to stay hidden. I shouldn't be this upset over him not talking to me, right? I told him that we can't happen, so he is giving me what I want. But I can't stop wondering why he's stopped fighting for this to happen between us. Why now?

I follow him up the stairs and see only one bedroom door is open, and Ace is standing in the doorway in just his jeans. He's taken off his socks, boots and shirt.

"Ace, which room am I in?"

"This one," he states without turning to face me.

"Wait—what?" I stammer.

"I said you're staying in my bed with me. You don't come into my house and sleep in another bed." He did not just say that. I can't sleep next to him.

Oh, God.

My heartrate spikes and I start to panic. I haven't shared a bed with a man since Gary. My vision gets blurry and my breathing is coming in short, fast pants. My knees go weak, but Ace catches me before they completely give out.

"I got you, baby. Just breathe for me. In and out. In and out, that's it. Good girl." His voice is calming and soothing. My breathing settles and I see that I'm in Ace's lap in the middle of the bed. He's leaning against the large, wooden headboard.

I raise my head up and take in Ace's worried expression. Without thinking, I lift my hand and smooth the creases between his eyebrows.

"Don't frown. You're too handsome for that." My words must make him happy because he smiles and leans in to kiss me. This time I let it happen. I slide my hand around his neck and feel the short hair under my fingertips.

Wow, he can kiss.

He makes me forget all the bad that has happened—not only today but over the last few years. I lose myself in the touch of his lips, in the way his tongue mates with mine. I feel his hands slide up and down my thighs and find myself hating the jeans I'm wearing.

My skin is heating up, but then Ace speaks, and it's like an ice-cold bucket of water is poured over me.

"Fucking hell, sweetheart, you're a fucking blessing to me." I freeze and pull back. My body jerks from his and I clamber off the bed. I shake my head back and forth making myself slightly dizzy. I know my hair looks crazy right now, but I don't care.

"Ana, what—" I stop him.

"This *cannot happen*," I scream, and wrap my arms around my stomach, somehow trying to protect myself.

"Why? You know I want you, and I know you want me. I will never hurt you, Ana. Fuck. Tell me, why? You never open up to me. You never talk to me. *Why?*" He roars the last word, making me flinch and fall against the wall before sliding to the floor.

My gentle crying has now become full on sobs. Ace has never once scared me, but right now he is. I'm shaking like a leaf. I feel a shadow fall over me and shrink back even more. I hear a growl, and my head snaps toward the sound.

Ace is now standing by the bed, pulling his t-shirt back over his body. He picks up his phone and presses a few buttons before placing it to his ear.

"I need you at my place. ASAP." Then he hangs up. I watch him get his boots back on through my hair, and don't stop the tears from running down my face. I hiccup and Ace casts me a side glance before standing to full height and stepping towards the bedroom door. He looks down at me and speaks.

"I would never hurt you, babe. Seeing you cower from me is breaking my heart but fuck if I can look at you right now. Court is coming over to watch you. He'll take you home tomorrow so you can get ready for work." With that, he walks out.

My body shakes with sobs. It's getting harder to breathe, but I force a deep breath. I can't pass out again. The last time that happened I woke up in the hospital with a broken arm and a concussion.

I must have fallen asleep, because suddenly I'm being lifted and carried towards Ace's bed. I freak out.

"NO! Not his bed," I scream.

"Okay, Mouse, chill the fuck out, woman. Fucking hell. I'll take you to the spare room. He can deal with your crazy arse tomorrow."

Court lays me on the bed and I'm asleep in no time, the events of the day clearly having taken a toll on my body and mind.

When I wake up, the sun is shining through the window because no one closed the curtains. I peel my eyes open and notice I am not in my bedroom. I shoot up to a sitting position and take in the room

You can tell this is a man's bedroom. The walls are white, the curtains are navy. There is a chest of drawers, with a large TV on top, plus a matching wardrobe. Two bedside tables match the other furniture.

I close my eyes as last night's events come flooding back, and a sob breaks through. I cover my face with my hand and cry.

Taking a few breaths, I climb off the bed and walk out of the room, looking for a bathroom. I need to empty my bladder. I pass Ace's room and see the bedding looks like it did last night, which means he didn't come home after our incident. My stomach clenches and I continue my search for the bathroom. Once I find it, I do my business and wash my hands and face.

I pull up my big girl knickers and walk down the stairs. Court is sitting at the large, round, six-seater kitchen table, drinking a mug of coffee. He lifts his head when he hears me. Court is a mean man, but he's good-looking, and he only sleeps with girls once. I've heard this way too many times to count, but the females flock to his broody demeanour.

"I'm gonna go. I've called an Uber," I lie. I just want to get out of here.

"I'll take you. I have the van." I shake my head, but Court is having none of it. He stands to his full height, towering over me. His thick black beard and piercing green eyes stare down at me.

"Fine." I know when to not argue with these men. I pick up my phone and bag and follow him out of Ace's house. I take one more look around because I know I won't be coming back here again. I pushed Ace too far last night.

I'm not sure if that's a good thing or a bad thing.

I'm in the kitchen finishing up placing some of the dinner orders when I hear his voice. My heart skips a beat and my muscles tense up. I haven't seen or heard from him in three days. Nancy just told me he was busy with the club and would be around soon. I know he's had eyes on us because a prospect called Ditch had been in the cafe every day, watching over us. He got his name because he's been run off the road and into a ditch quite a few times. I laughed when he explained his name.

I pick up the plates and take them out to the counter for Alesha, Bull's old lady. She smiles at me when I set the plates down, then shakes her head.

"Can you take these over to the boys, please?" She points to the table where EC, Batch and Ace are sitting. I go to shake my head, but she gives me a stern look. I huff out breath and pick the plates up, scowling at her. She just laughs at me. Why doesn't anyone believe I can be mean? I step up to the table and the boys' conversation stops. Yeah, because that's not awkward.

"Here you go." I set the two plates down in front of Batch and EC and turn to walk away, but his voice stops me.

"Can I order?" I take a deep breath before turning around to face the man who has held my mind captive for the last three days—hell, who am I kidding, for the last year.

"What's the magic word?" I raise an eyebrow at him. I know Nancy brought him up better than that.

"Now." He smirks at me.

"Whatever." I walk away but stop when he calls my name. I can see people are watching our interaction.

"Please. Can I place an order?"

"Of course. You know where the counter is," I smart off, and speed walk back into the kitchen. I can hear the boys laughing it up. I feel proud of myself for not breaking under his stare. He was the one who walked away from me. I know I hurt his feelings, but he scared the ever-loving crap out of me. I was only trying to put distance between us. He's a scary biker who can have any woman he wants, so why me? I'm damaged goods, as they say. Gary has ruined me for everyone.

"Oh, you think that was funny?" Ace's voice comes from the kitchen door. I jump and place a hand over my rapidly beating heart.

"You scared me. Will you stop creeping up on me like a flippin' ninja or something." I chuckle but Ace's face shows no emotion.

Oh great, here we go.

"It wasn't nice to show me up in front of my boys like that, babe."

"Oh, so I'm 'babe' again. Nice to know. I didn't mean to show you up, Ace, but Nancy brought you up with manners. Biker or not, you can still use them," I state to him. Manners were a big thing in our house growing up.

Manners cost nothing.

"Fuck, you're never going to make things easy, are you?"

"Easy? For what?"

"Us, Ana."

"There is no 'us', Ace," I say, emphasising my point with

finger quotes. He sighs and rubs his beard, and really naughty thoughts flash in my head of the way he would feel between my legs.

"There will be—"

Screaming and yelling pull us from the moment. We both dash out to the cafe and see Nancy laying on the floor, unconscious. We both run to her side. I can see Ditch is already on the phone. I can only assume he's dialling nine-nine-nine for an ambulance.

"Mum, can you hear me? Mum?" Ace's frantic voice fills the space. I pull my cardigan off my shoulders and bundle it up under her head. I check her pulse and find it's there, but slow.

"Ambulance is on the way, Ace," Ditch says from somewhere. Ace just nods but never takes his eyes off his mum. Ditch will make a good brother one day.

"She will be fine, Ace. She's a fighter," I tell him. He nods but doesn't look at me. I only hope what I'm saying is true.

Ace

I'm pacing the hallway right outside my mother's hospital room. They have been in there for what seems like days, but I know it's only been a few hours. Fuck. The boys are sitting in the waiting room as only immediate family are allowed back here. Once we know what's going on, I'll let them know.

Ana is here with me. She keeps offering me reassuring smiles, but I can't bring myself to believe they will make everything better.

The door opens and a nurse steps out. She smiles at me in a sympathetic way, and my heart sinks into my boots.

"You can come in now, Mr McGowan." I feel a small, warm hand slip into my cold, callused one. I don't need to turn to look in order to know who it is.

"I'm here." I squeeze her hand and walk into the room. My mum looks so fucking small. And pale. Did she really look like that yesterday when I saw her? Mum smiles at me, but when she sees Ana's hand in mine, she beams. Tears fill her eyes at the sight of us together. I know she wants us together; she's made that known for fucking months.

"Mum." I lean in and kiss her head, keeping one hand

wrapped around Ana's tiny one. "You scared the fuck out of me —of us."

I ignore the doctors in the room and solely focus on my mother. Tears fill her eyes. I lean in and kiss her head, while still holding Ana's hand. She's my lifeline at the moment; she's keeping me from lashing out with the anger that's coursing through my veins.

"I'm sorry, my boy. My body just isn't strong enough anymore. You need to know a few things. I need to tell you some secrets that I've been keeping from you."

"What secrets?"

"Let the doctors talk first, okay?" I nod. Why do I feel I am *not* going to like whatever the fuck they're going to say. *Motherfucker.*

"Mr. McGowan, there isn't much else we can do for your mother at this time. She is refusing any and all treatments. So all we can do for her is to keep her as pain free as possible, and comfortable."

"What the fuck do you mean *as pain free as possible*? I want her completely fucking pain free," I snap. I feel Ana squeeze her fingers around mine, but I snatch my hand out of hers and walk towards the window. I close my eyes and breathe in and out through my nose, trying to calm my anger.

I feel Ana come up behind me and run her hand over my back, her touch burning me, and I snap.

"Fuck off, Ana. Fuck, just leave me alone, for just a second. *Fuck!*" I hear her gasp but don't turn around to face her. I can see the pain I just caused. My anger spikes and I spin around to face the people in the room. My mother is looking disappointed in me. I don't look at Ana—I can't bring myself to do it.

"I need to get the fuck out of here. I'll leave the boys here and come back in a bit." I walk over to my mum and kiss her head. "I love you, Mum."

"Ace, don't go," she pleads. But I need to clear my head.

"I'll be back." I leave the room and stop once I reach the boys.

"Watch over them. I need to get out of here." I get a nod from Dyson and leave them there.

Stalking out of the hospital, my anger is raging through me. I need to get on my baby and feel the wind on my face. I reach my bike and climb on before starting her up. Pulling out of the car park, I see the building that is keeping my dying mother alive get smaller and smaller in the side mirrors.

I drive for hours, going nowhere in particular. The wind is whipping around me, my sunglasses shading my eyes from the sunset I'm driving towards. The sun feels warm on my face, and I can't stop from smiling. My mum loves sitting out in the garden at this time of the day. She says we should enjoy at least one sunset in our lives, as we never know when it will be our last day on earth.

I pull over at a service station because I need a piss. I've been driving for hours. I empty my bladder and stop to grab a coffee and a bite to eat. I watch as the people come and go from this place. Seeing different people live their lives while my mother's life is about to end... I huff out a breath and walk back to my bike.

I take a deep breath and walk into my mother's hospital room. I hate the smell of these rooms. My mother lays on the bed looking smaller than before. I hate seeing her like this. There are tubes everywhere, wires coming from every direction. The heart monitor beeps, filling the room. Stepping closer to the bed, I take my mum's tiny, withered hand in my strong one.

I lift my gaze to the chair in the corner. My Ana is curled up in a ball, her head resting on her bent arm. Her hair has fallen over half of her face. She looks like a fucking angel sleeping there. My gut tightens as I remember the way I spoke to her earlier. She will be pissed at me, but I won't let her fester in those feelings. I'll apologize, and we can move past it.

"Honey." Mum's weak voice comes from her bed, barely a whisper. I almost miss it.

"Hey, Mum. How are you feeling?" I lean in and kiss her cheek. She smells like oranges; the one piece of food she managed to eat.

"Like I'm dying." She smiles weakly at me.

"Fucking hell." I pinch the bridge of my nose.

"Too soon?" she jokes. I can't help but chuckle. She pats the side of the bed. "Come sit." I perch on the bed and take her hand in mine. I bend my knee and rest our hands on it.

"I'm sorry I left. I'm a fucking arsehole, Mum. I'm so fucking sorry—but hearing what the doc was saying..." I take a deep breath. "I couldn't handle it. Which is shitty, because it's you who's going through all this shit."

"I know, Ace. It's a lot to take in, but we will deal with this. My time here is limited, and I don't want to see you being angry in my last few days." My head snaps up to her face, and she gives me a sympathetic smile and a nod.

"Days?" My voice cracks as the emotion tries to break through. I'm a fucking hard arse, unless it involves the women in my life. I go to climb off the bed, but Mum stops me. She takes the corner of my cut in her hand.

"I need to tell you everything. I understand if you hate me after this, but I need to tell you. I have waited way too long to open up about this." Tears fill her eyes, and she takes a shuddering breath.

"Mum, I could never hate you." She nods, unconvinced.

"You have a brother, Ace. A twin. His name is Aiden." My heart slams into my chest and my breath catches.

"A brother? A fucking twin? What the fuck, Mum?" I force out, my anger rising again. I know I can't lash out at her.

I could never hate her, but fucking hell—a twin brother. Why has she kept this from me?

"Tell me," I grind out between my clenched teeth, trying to control my rage and confusion.

"I met your father one summer, and we just... clicked. I was working in a bakery at the time, and he came in. We flirted at first, but things quickly escalated. I fell hard and fast, and so did he. He was a prospect at the time... I fell pregnant with you and Aiden shortly after we got together. He was great—until he became a fully-patched member."

"My father is a member of an MC?" I shake my head, trying to sort through what she's telling me.

"Yes. He became the president when you and Aiden were young—toddler age. He changed right after, staying out all night. When I questioned him he would yell at me, tell me the club came first and I should shut up and deal with it." He sounds like an absolute cunt.

"Did he ever hit you?"

She nods. "He did. I took it until you boys were three-years-old. I made plans to get away from him and take you both with me. But I failed—I failed you both." She sobs into her hand—the one I'm not holding.

"You didn't fail us, Mum. Would I have liked to know I had a twin brother? Fuck yeah. But I understand why you left; my father sounds like a complete wanker." That makes Mum chuckle.

"He was. That day, I had it all planned out. But it all went to hell when your father came home early from his other girl's house because Aiden fell ill at nursery and had to come home." So, my father claimed an old lady and had two fucking kids, and he was fucking around on her. Holy fuck, I am so fucking glad she got rid of that piece of shit.

"I had you in the car and was getting ready to pick up Aiden when Trevor came storming over to me and told me to leave, take you, and go. I cried and asked him to let me leave with you both."

"Let me guess... He threatened us, didn't he?" Tears are streaming down her ghost-white cheeks.

"He did. He told me to either leave Aiden with him, or he would kill the three of us. I had no choice, Ace. I had to leave him. I couldn't risk either of you getting hurt, or worse." I move towards her and hug her shrinking body, fearful I might hug her too tight and hurt her. The emotions running around my body are nowhere near what I imagine my mum has felt all these years, hiding this from me.

"I'm so sorry, baby boy. So sorry." My mother sobs into my t-shirt. I hold her as tight as I can without causing her pain.

"You have nothing to be sorry for. Where is Aiden now?" I release her and go to wipe her eyes, when a tissue appears at my right. I jump a little, seeing Ana standing there. She offers me a small smile, and I take the tissue from her and dry my mother's face.

"Thanks," I tell her. She nods and steps back towards her chair, but I snag her wrist and tug her gently, signalling I want her to stay by my side. Our eyes stay locked as Ana closes the small distance between us. She must see my need for her written all over my face, because she settles at my side, leaning her body against mine and resting a hand around my waist, stroking the leather.

I take her kindness and warmth, even though I don't deserve it after the way I treated her earlier. I was a fucking prick to her. I wouldn't blame her if she kicked me in the balls.

"Your brother..." she takes a deep breath, "is a member of The Cornish Crusaders. I believe they're a good club. Your father... is dead, Ace. He was a good for nothing man, anyway. Look at what he did to us." I take in the relief that the fucker is already dead.

"I'm glad he's already six foot under, because I would have fucking ripped that man apart piece by fucking piece." I take a deep breath. "So, I need to go to Cornwall then, yeah?" I need to meet my brother. I shift slightly and wrap my arms around her waist, we are at the perfect height for me to do this with ease.

"Yes, go. See him, meet him. You both missed out on so much, honey. Do this for me. Do it for you both." I nod in agreement, knowing she's right. I do need to do this. I owe it to my mother to try and get my brother to come here and meet her. Does he know about her? If he did, why didn't he come looking for her?

"Okay, Mum. I'll go this weekend. That gives me a few days with you before I go down to get him and bring him home to you. You need to meet him too."

"No, Ace. Just you. Seeing me may hurt him, and I don't ever want to do that." My heart aches for my mother. My brother should meet her before she...she... Motherfucker, I can't say it.

"We'll see." Her eyes slowly close, showing her exhaustion. I sigh and gently move Ana away from me, so I can kiss the top of my mum's head. I step back and drop my body into the chair next to the bed. Ana takes her chair in the corner. I watch her, while she watches my mother. Ana always wears her heart on her sleeve, and she's showing how much she will miss Mum. Her eyes look like glass orbs in the light, filled with tears ready to fall.

My mother has had to live her life not seeing one of her children, not knowing what happened to him. Wondering if he is just like my father, or if he is his own man. I pray to fuck that Aiden is not a wanker like our father. I will lay the fucker out if he is.

Seeing Ana look like a woman who has the weight of the world on her shoulders makes my heart want her more. I've wanted her since I first saw her, but she always held me at arm's length. Fuck, she held me a mile away. Something is going on with her past and I will figure it out.

"You okay?" I ask her. She nods but doesn't speak. "How is Zarah?" I try again. I want her to talk to me. I need to fucking apologise for the shit that went down earlier.

"She's okay—still sore, but like she said: she's alive." I nod, my gut tightening because I need to man the fuck up now.

"Listen, I was a bastard earlier. I shouldn't have reacted the way I did. None of this is your fault. So, I'm sorry. Take it because I don't say I'm sorry often." I chuckle—to myself more than her.

"Take it?" Her eyes are wide with shock.

"Yep."

"God, you really are a poxy idiot, Ace McGowan. I understand why you were upset earlier, and yeah, I forgive you, but for you to sit there and have the cheek to tell me I need to *take* your apology... You have another thing coming if you think that will happen." I smirk at her; seeing her riled up is a fucking turn on. My dick jerks in my jeans, and I adjust him. In front of her.

She gasps and looks out the window.

"What? You can't expect my cock not to react to your feistiness coming through. Baby, you are hot as fuck when you're pissed."

"I—I'm not pissed, Ace. God."

"Yeah, babe, you are, and I fucking love it. You're not normally this talkative with me. It takes so much effort to get you to speak to me. I'm so used to short, quick answers. This..." I wave my hand back and forth between us, "is fucking amazing. I need and want more. From today, you will talk to me, no ifs or buts. You will talk to me. I want to know every-fucking-thing you and your sister are hiding from me. No more."

"No more what?" she asks, shifting her gaze back to mine.

"Waiting." I leave it at that.

Five

Ace

My hands grip the handlebars on my bike, turning the skin white. My breathing is tight, and my chest feels like a ton of cement has been poured over me. I look to the service station, willing Ana to walk through the automatic doors and help me breathe again.

Seven days ago, my mother, the woman who gave me life, took her last breath. The fucking reaper came and took her from me. From all of us. She got weaker and weaker as the hours passed. It was fucking crushing to see her slowly die in front of me. The club was in the room with her. The doctors told us she was too weak to move, to take home, so they let everyone who could fit into her room be there.

The boys brought Zarah down to her room to say goodbye. I'm glad she was there, because Ana needed her. The room was filled with a group of men in denim and leather. The nurses didn't know what to do with us, so they let us be.

I sat on the bed, with one arm slung over the back of Mum's bed, waiting for her to slip away. I stroked the side of her face, taking in all the contact I could get before she left us. We talked some more about my brother, and little tidbits here and there between her sleeping.

The silence in the room was suffocating.

And deafening at the same time.

To be fair to the doctors and nurses, they didn't fiddle with Mum a lot. They let her be and allowed her to spend time with us. Then at nine-twenty-three p.m., Nancy Harris passed away. The best woman I have ever had the pleasure of having in my life. The best woman I could have asked to be my mum. My fucking world.

Mum's funeral is in three days, so here I am, almost at my brother's clubhouse. I really had hoped Aiden could have met Mum before she passed, but shit happens, and she was too fucking tired to hold on.

Ana finally walks out of the double doors and heads for me. I can tell she's been crying again because her eyes are red. She offers me the cup of coffee, and I take it without words.

"Do you want to talk about it?" she asks. Ana has shown she's no longer afraid to talk to me since that night in the hospital. I told her no more waiting around for her to get used to me. I haven't told her she's mine yet—I will ease her into that—but I think she has some kind of clue.

I take her hand and lead her over to the picnic bench off to the left. I make her sit next to me, so I can keep her close and smell her perfume or whatever the shit it is she sprays on her body.

I lean in and smell her neck. She stiffens a little but doesn't pull away.

"I would rather talk about you, babe. Tell me about my girl." I growl into her neck as her scent makes my cock thicken in my jeans. My legs are straddling the bench, and I close in on Ana, so my legs are pretty much caging her in. I love having her here; it feels so fucking right.

But what I wouldn't give for her to be straddling me and taking my cock fast and hard...

"Fuck," I mutter, and breathe out. "You drive my cock fucking crazy. When are you going to let me between these creamy thighs, baby?" A gasp comes from her and she tries to move back from me.

"Ace." My name leaves her lips in a whisper but also sounds all breathy. Yeah, she likes the dirty talk. Good to know.

"What? I told you no more waiting. But we'll talk more after I deal with today, and Mum's funeral." I kiss the skin behind her ear and she shivers. I need to change the subject before I take her hard and fast here in front of everyone.

"Drink up so we can hit the road." We finish our coffee, people-watching in silence, before we get on the road and deal with the shit storm I'm sure will come our way.

I pull up outside the Cornish Crusaders MC clubhouse. It's your typical clubhouse, a prospect on the gate, and I remove my helmet and turn to him.

"I'm here to see Aiden. Get him for me," I demand. I need to show dominance here, otherwise they'll think I'm a fucking pussy.

"Who are you?" the little prick asks.

"Boy, don't fuck with me. Do what you're fucking told."

"Ace, be nice," Ana whispers from behind me.

"Fuck nice, babe." I look back at the prospect and cock an eyebrow. Fucker knows what I want. He radios through, and I see a group of men come towards us. All in leather and denim, just like me.

I spot him in the middle. There is no fucking way in hell he can he deny we're brothers; we look almost identical.

Ana gasps behind me, and I turn my head to look at her. Her hand is covering her mouth in shock.

"Hey," he says.

"Aiden?" I say his name.

"Who the hell are you?" he asks, sounding pissed and ready to throat punch me.

"I'm Ace." I hold my hand out for him to shake. I may be a bad-arse biker, but Mum brought me up with manners to use when needed.

"What do you want?" He folds his arms and stands just like I do. Shoulders tight, legs spread apart. It's a defence stance I use to intimidate people. My heart pounds in my chest.

"Umm..." I look back at Ana. She gives me a reassuring nod, and I turn back to the biker standing in front of me, who thinks he's scaring me. "Can we maybe talk?" I ask him. But if he's anything like me, he'll want his brother at his back for this. He doesn't know me from Adam, so he doesn't trust me, even though I am him, in retrospect. I feel Ana's hand on the small of my back, and my chest expands.

"Go ahead."

"In private," I respond.

"How the hell do you know who I am?" Aiden grinds out, his jaw clenching.

"I'll tell you. Can we go somewhere—where I can explain it all?" I ask again. I'm asking, even though I know he's a stubborn fuckhead and won't budge.

"No, you tell me now. How do you know me?" he asks again, getting pissed at me, but fuck if I care.

"I'm your brother," I state.

"You're lying. I don't have a brother." He doesn't stick around to listen to what I have to say. He turns to the woman next to him and steers her towards the clubhouse. I need this prick to listen to me, for fucks sake.

"Please. Our parents are Trevor McGowan and Nancy Harris. You're my twin brother, Aiden."

The woman next to him gasps and snaps her head to look at him, then back to me, and asks,

"Is it true?"

"Yeah. I only found out about Aiden a week ago. I didn't know he existed."

"Babe, let's go home and talk to them." Clearly she's his woman, going by the way she's touching him. Aiden nods and we head out to their place, Ana on the back of my bike again, making my dick hard in this very awkward situation.

We pull up outside their house and the woman calls to us, "Come on in."

I place my hand on the small of Ana's back and guide her into the house. We both sit on the couch, barely touching. Ana is still very unsure of what's happening between us, but fuck me, once this shit is over with, she will know who the fuck she belongs to. We've wasted so much time already. But no more. No-fucking-more.

"I'll get some tea." Before she can step out of the room, Aiden grips her hand and speaks.

"Flower, not everyone drinks tea."

"We're fine, honestly. Don't trouble yourself," I say. I need a fucking whiskey not fucking tea, but I won't say anything because she is being polite, plus she seems to be my brother's woman. My brother. Fucking hell, it still feels weird having that shit racing around my head.

Aiden speaks. "Come and sit, flower."

"I want some tea," she whines, but not in an annoying way.

"I'll make you some tea. Please, sit down," Aiden tells her. A look passes between them: love and adoration.

"Is everything okay?" I ask them. Is she ill? Oh shit, and I'm about to tell him about our mum. She sits on the couch and kicks off her shoes, before tucking her legs under her arse.

"Yeah, your brother thinks that me being pregnant means I can't lift a kettle." She shoots a glare at him, but he ignores her and walks into the kitchen.

"How far along are you?" Ana asks from my side.

"Oh, sorry. This is my friend, Ana." I introduce them.

"I'm fifteen weeks. I've got a long way to go yet," she explains to us, raising her voice. I can only guess to make sure Aiden hears her. I look at Ana and down to her stomach. My mind spins with thoughts of her barefoot and pregnant in my kitchen, or at the compound, making sure every fucker knows she's pregnant with my baby. I shake my head when Ana speaks.

"Ah, that's great. Congratulations." Aiden walks back in and places her mug of tea on the coffee table in front of us. "Ah, how sweet. He's already bought you a 'Mum' mug."

"No, we already have a son," she explains. We sit in a few minutes of very fucking awkward silence until Ana elbows me. I look and frown at her, and she subtly nods, telling me to start talking.

"Yeah, so... Um, I'm not really sure how to say this, so I'm just gonna say it." I rub my hands together, my palms sweating like a bitch in heat. "Our mum died last week." I take a deep breath, forcing the emotion down for now.

"Oh, no," gasps Aiden's woman. She moves closer to him and takes his hand in hers. I carry on and explain all this painful shit that I have been through enough times already, but he needs this.

"She had breast cancer. She found a lump and never got it checked out. Before she died, she told me about you."

"She ran off and left me." Aiden's anger shines through. I guess I can't blame the bloke for that.

"Yeah, she told me. She explained that her plan was to take us both. She had money stashed away from our dad—"

He cuts me off, anger radiating from him. "Don't call him that," he snaps. "He doesn't deserve a title like that." His woman touches his hand, calming him. Ana does that to me, not that she knows it. Yet.

"Sorry, I don't remember him. Mum said he used to beat her. That she had one chance to get away, and she took it. She didn't think you would be sent home from nursery, let alone that our father would pick you up."

"Why didn't she come back for him?" Flower asks.

I answer her. "She tried. He—threatened her. He said if she came near him again, he would kill her and me. She was scared. She had all these photos of you; she kept a close eye on you whenever she could. She asked me to tell you that she loved you, and she was sorry."

"Sorry?" Aiden bites out. His face is red, and he's one angry-looking fucker, but he doesn't scare me. Fuck, it's the look I see when I'm pissed and catch a glimpse of my reflection. He paces the floor and runs his hand over his beard. I snort, thinking it must be a twin thing, because I do that when I'm stressed or pissed.

"She left me with a man who beat me—repeatedly. I had the worst life."

"Aiden." I say his name, getting his attention.

"Solar. My name is Solar," he growls at me.

"Come on, man. We're brothers—twins," I retort. His face twists in anger as he spits his words at me.

"No, my brothers are the guys back at that club. The ones who have always been there for me!" he screams at me.

"Aiden." His woman gives him a warning tone as she climbs to her feet and places her tiny hands on his chest. To my utter shock, he nods at her.

"I think it's a good idea if we let this information settle in and talk later. Are you guys staying around here?" Flower asks.

"Yeah, we'll find a hotel or something," Ana says, and comes to stand at my side. She slides her hand in mine, and I feel my skin prickle from the touch.

"If you write your number down, we'll give you a call tomorrow," Flower says, but Aiden just stands there, staring at nothing. I can only imagine all this shit running around his head. He's like me; he needs to sort through everything before he makes a decision. I drop my gaze to Ana, bent over the coffee table, scribbling her number down.

"Thank you," Ana's soft voice says.

I look at my brother and offer him a nod, which he returns. I take Ana's hand and lead her out of the house and over to my bike. I hand her helmet over and watch as she puts it on.

"That went well," she quips. I chuckle and swing my leg over my bike.

"Yeah, as well as a priest saying no to a fucking stripper." She climbs on the back of the bike, wrapping her slender arms around my waist.

"Thanks for coming with me," I say, running my fingers over her hands locked at my waist.

"I wanted to come with you, Ace. I do care for you. Now let's get a hotel, okay? I'm kinda tired after riding all day."

"Thanks anyway. Yeah, I'm kinda beat myself. Let's go and get some sleep."

I drive us around town until I find a hotel for the night. Ana makes me book a twin room, which pisses me off. I want her in a bed with me, her arse pressed up against my dick. I bet her body will fit fucking perfect against mine.

I get a text asking if I'll meet Solar the next morning in a coffee shop in town. Of course, I agree. We need to get this shit over with.

Sleeping in the same room as Ana and not being able to touch her is killing me. She showered, and that was hell all on its own. The thought of her wet and smooth and soapy sent my cock into overdrive. I'm going to fuck her senseless when we get home and have time to talk about us. Well, I'm going to talk; she's going to listen.

Ana Dawkins is going to be mine. End of fucking story.

Ana

WE ARRIVE AT THE COFFEE SHOP AND MY HEART THUMPS IN MY chest. Solar is a scary guy. So much like Ace, in a way, but Ace never scares me. He held my hand when we climbed off the bike, and even held the door open for me. Nancy taught him well.

Solar and his girlfriend are sitting at a table, but Solar stands when he sees us enter the cafe.

"I'm sorry about yesterday, it all just came as a bit of a shock. I didn't introduce you properly. This is Jasmine, my old lady." Jasmine gets to her feet, giving Ace a hug.

"It's nice to see you both again," she says, before hugging me. We all sit back down, just as a waitress comes over to take our orders.

"What club are you with?" Solar asks Ace.

"The Unforgiven Riders. We're not far from here, only in Torquay. How long have you been a member?"

"Fourteen years now. You?" he asks.

"Same. Mum bought me my first bike when I was sixteen and I prospected until I was eighteen. Now I'm Sergeant-at-Arms." Pride laces his voice. We go quiet, while the waitress places our food down on the table.

I speak after a brief silence. "Nancy's funeral is in three days. It would be great if you could come, both of you." I offer a sympathetic smile at Solar. His eyes flick between Ace and me, but he doesn't speak.

"Thank you. We'll—" Jasmine is cut off by Solar.

"We'll discuss it."

"We've gotta head back today. Get everything sorted," Ace explains. "I'd really like it if we could stay in touch. Maybe get to know each other. I'd like to meet your son, too, at some point."

"That would be nice. Nate would love that, wouldn't he, Aiden?" Jasmine chimes in, trying to get Solar to relax and get to know his brother.

"How old is he?" Ace asks Jasmine.

"Five," she replies.

"Wow, you guys have been together a while, then," I query.

"Not long enough," Solar puts in.

"Thanks for agreeing to talk with me," Ace says to Solar as they both stand.

"Thanks for coming to find me." The two brothers shake hands.

Jasmine adds,

"We'll let you know about the funeral." We both stand with them, and Ace slides his arm around my shoulders and leads me out of the cafe. His touches are getting bolder and more frequent these days. I know he wants more, but it scares the hell out of me.

But Ace being Ace, he always gets what he wants. I don't know what tomorrow will bring and losing Nancy has made me look at things differently. Well, it's made my heart and body look at things differently, but my head... that's a different story. My head knows how much Ace can hurt me. My heart won't take the pain he will inflict on me if things go bad.

I'll have to move again, leave behind the cafe, the friends I have made here, and possibly my sister. Zarah has made a life here, just as much as me. She has her own friends now. I would hate to take that away from her. But I could never stick around if things ended badly for Ace and me.

Speaking of Zarah... My phone rings and her face pops up on the screen.

"Hey, sis," I answer.

"Hey. How did things go?" I look over to Ace, who's leaning against his bike, his ankles crossed, as well as his arms, with his phone in hand.

He is one sexy man, that's for sure. I lick my lips and fall into my 'Ace Daze', as Zarah calls it. I think about the way his hands would feel on me. Would his beard scratch and mark my skin when he's—

"ANA!" My name is screamed through the phone, followed by a chuckle. "Are you in your 'Ace Daze' again?"

"No. What are you talking about?" I lift my thumb to my mouth and nibble on the nail—a nervous habit. Nancy used to slap my hand when she saw me doing it.

"Mmmhmm, I bet you're standing there looking like a creeper, staring at Ace McGowan. Am I right?" I blush, even though I know she can't see me.

"No!" My voice comes a little high-pitched, catching Ace's attention. He smirks, and then winks at me, making my blush deepen beyond belief. I spin and turn away from him, trying to calm the raging blood rushing around my body. He knows what he does to me—hell, to every woman who comes into contact with him.

"Porkies, Smallie. So how was it?"

"How was what?" I ask.

"The meeting with the brother. Girl, what did you think I was talking about?" I look over my shoulder at Ace and see he's now talking to a woman, who looks more his type. I watch as she runs her fingers down his forearm, tracing his tattoos, and he lets her.

My stomach drops, and my 'inner Ana' pipes in, telling me she knew she was right about him all along.

I turn my back to them, not wanting to see their flirting, and answer my sister.

"It was okay. Aiden was shocked at first, but Ace explained everything. He has a son and an old lady to think about, but they might come to the funeral. So, we'll see."

"That's good, then—that he accepted Ace. So when are you guys coming back?"

I look over my shoulder just in time to see Ace throw his head back in laughter at something the woman said. Bile rises in my throat, but I swallow it back down. How embarrassing it would be for me to vomit not only on a very public street, but in front on Ace.

"Soon. I want these last few days over with," I state, and walk towards the corner shop to grab some water. Ace is still talking to the woman and hasn't noticed that I've moved. He just proved me bloody right, didn't he.

"What's happened between you and Ace?" Zarah enquires.

"Nothing, and nothing will ever happen. I mean it Z, nothing." I hear her sigh on the other end of the phone before she speaks again.

"You have to move on, babe. You need a life that doesn't revolve around the cafe... or me. I want you to be happy."

"I am happy. I'm fine just as I am. How are you feeling anyway?" I ask, changing the subject. I'm done with the subject of Ace and me, because that is never going to happen.

"I'm okay, still a little sore. The cafe is doing great without you —just saying. So you can stay another night or two if you want." She sniggers.

"Whatever. I don't want to stay another night; I want to come home." I hang up on her, then pay for my drink before walking back to the bike, Ace and the woman still freaking talking.

I huff and stop at the back of the bike. My scowl shows Ace

I'm not happy with him, and the smile drops from his face for a split second before he snaps it back into place.

"Ana, this is Daisy. She was just telling me how she loves to *ride* motorbikes." I cross my arms and look her up and down. She is pretty, in a fake way, I suppose. Long blonde hair flowing down her back, boobs hanging out of the little halter top she's wearing, painted on jeans.

"Good for her. So, are you taking her for a ride? If so, I can call a taxi to get me home," I smart. I am never like this; he brings this out in me. I'm always the calm, collected one. I never let anything faze me anymore. Life is too short to be worrying over little things.

Ace's face is a picture. He looks shocked but amused by my outburst. I am so over the biker thing today.

"Oh, I know a good taxi firm for you. Let me get you the number," the woman pipes in. I look between her and Ace, his face now showing he's pissed at me. Well, what the hell did he expect?

"Oh, thanks, that would be fab. I'm sure Ace would love to take you for a ride. Ace likes to show the ladies what he has." I can't seem to stop my mouth from running away with itself.

"Ana." He says my name with a warning tone. I look to him again and see his eyes are narrowed on me, but Ace McGowan doesn't scare me.

"What? I'm being a good wingman—well wingwoman, but you get the gist of it." I shrug. I know I should stop, but my brain and mouth are no longer working in tandem.

"Ana, I really fucking suggest you shut the fuck up, right now." I ignore him and look to Daisy, who is still scrolling through her phone.

"Do you have that number for me?"

"ANA!" Ace barks my name, making both of us jump. My gaze snaps to his, and so does Daisy's. We enter a staring contest, one I know Ace will win. He has that broody stare down to a pat. I get lost in his eyes; they pull me in and hold me captive. My heart-beat spikes, and my body tingles from his penetrating gaze.

"Found it." Daisy's voice breaks the spell. Ace snaps his gaze to hers and growls his reply.

"She doesn't need a fucking taxi. I'm taking her home. She's the only one allowed on the back of my bike. So fuck off." She jumps a little but schools her features.

"You don't have to be an arsehole about it. If you want to shag Little Miss Prim, just say so. Flipping hell, mate, just shag her already and stop leading women like me on."

"Women like you? Bitch, women like you spread their legs for any man who shows interest. I know women like you; I have fucked women like you. But no more. You see this woman?" He points to me. "She is more woman than all of you slags put together. She has fucking self-respect, and integrity. Now again: *Piss off.*" He finishes his rant yelling at her.

"ACE!" I scold him, but in true Ace style, nothing fazes him.

"Get on the bike, Ana. We're going home." He leaves no room for arguments. He slides his leg over the bike and starts the engine, not waiting for me to climb on. I put my hands on my hips and take a deep breath. I have seen a pissed off Ace before, but now he's a tad more than pissed off. Ace's voice makes me jump again.

"Bike, babe. Now." I shake my head and put the helmet on, then climb onto the bike. Ace waits until I'm situated behind him and my arms are secure around his waist before he shoots off down the road. Even in his pissed off mood, he still made sure I was safely on his bike.

The ride home was uneventful. We stopped once because I needed the toilet and Ace wanted a drink. We didn't speak. He was still pissed at me. Well I have news for him: I'm still pissed at him, too.

I climb off the bike outside my house and, without a word to him, remove my overnight bag from the saddlebag on his bike. I march up my front door. After digging my keys out of my bag, I put the key in the lock, only to have a large, tattooed hand stop my movements.

"Baby." His voice is gentler than it was earlier today, making me shiver. His warm breath touches my bare neck.

Closing my eyes and taking a deep breath, I wait for his next words. I expect him to still be pissed at me, but his words shock me, even though I have heard them time and time again.

"Today was fucked up. We *both* fucked up." I try to turn to face him and give him a piece of my mind, but he stops me. "Both. I shouldn't have talked to her; you shouldn't have walked off. Plus, you don't ever try to palm your man off on another woman. What were you thinking?"

"You aren't my man, so she had free rein over you," I whisper. Even as I speak the words, bile threatens to leave my stomach.

"I am your man, and you're my woman. I've told you this before. No more waiting, babe. We have wasted to much fucking time already. If losing Mum has taught me one thing, it's we don't have enough time on this earth to waste it. So this is us not wasting anymore time. I'll give you until after the funeral to see things my way." He pulls at my jacket so he can get to my bare neck, and lays gentle kisses there, sending a waterfall of emotions over my body.

His chest touches my back, and I can feel the heat seeping through his club jacket and into my body. The material does nothing to stop the connection between us.

"You are mine, Ana Dawkins." He lays another open-mouthed kiss to my neck before stepping away. "See you soon, babe." With that, he leaves me standing there like a fish out of water. I keep my back to him, until I hear the bike start. His voice startles me again. He really needs to stop doing that shit.

"Inside now, Ana." I open the door and quickly step inside. I stand at the threshold, looking at this sexy man sitting on his bike outside my house. The man that wants to claim me in every way.

Oh, lordy.

I give him a little wave and close the door. Once the door is fully closed, I hear his bike pull away and down the street. Again with my safety coming first.

It always seems to be first and last with Ace.

Seven

Ace

LEAVING ANA THE DAY WE GOT BACK FROM MEETING MY BROTHER was fucking hard, and by hard I mean my cock was hard as steel. The way she clung to me on the bike, and the way her body shivered when I told her she was mine and I was hers...

I was fucking livid with her when she tried telling that bimbo she could have me.

I know she's scared about what could happen between us, but fuck if I'm a selfish man and want her no matter what. She will open up to me. I will get her to submit to me. I chuckle to myself, remembering the way her body responded to me. Fuck, she has always responded to me.

"Hey, fucker." I hear my name being called as I walk into the clubhouse. EC is sitting by the bar with a club girl on his lap, her tits hanging out of her top, his other hand holding his phone.

"What?" I ask, as I make my way over.

"You got everything sorted for tomorrow?"

I nod, swallowing the lump in my throat. I may be a bad arse biker, but fuck, my mother was my world.

"Yeah, everything is done. Ana and Z are bringing the food over in the morning. We're shutting the cafe down. I wanted someone to do the catering, but Ana was having none of it. She's as stubborn as a fucking mule that one. What you up to?" I ask, nodding towards the phone. EC winks at me and turns the phone around so I can see the screen.

"SnatchChat," is all he says. I shake my head at him. It's a game all the boys play. Hell, even I did at one point. The boys like to share a picture of a girl's pussy when they're done fucking it. EC named it 'SnatchChat'.

"Put the bitch in her place, Ace. She should know she can't talk down to you. Skanks like her are fake as fuck, anyway. She's using the innocent act to reel you in. But I can give you what you want, baby. Anything," the club girl on EC's lap says.

"The fuck you say? You don't call my woman a bitch, or a fucking skank. You're the skank and whore around here, bitch. You're here for one reason and one reason only, you fucking get me?" I spit at her. Fucking cunt calling my woman names.

"Your—your woman? Since when?" she stammers, as EC, none too gently, gets her off his lap.

"Doesn't matter. No one slags off Mouse. Piss off," EC snaps at her.

"But, EC, I thought—"

"Well you thought fucking wrong. Ana belongs to Ace, so fucking deal with it and keep your trap shut." We both turn our back on her, and I signal to the prospect to bring me a beer.

We sit in silence for fuck knows how long, until that amazing silence is broken. "So you finally claimed her, huh?" EC speaks from my side. I nod. I've barely talked to Ana about it, but she knows it's coming. Well, she should know it's fucking coming.

I look over to see Suede sitting in his big, worn, leather chair with his old lady, Lola, sitting on his lap. They are Dyson's parents.

Suede's hands slide dangerously close to her pussy. No one here is shy about shagging in public and the boys here are not shy about their sexuality.

Take EC, that boy will fuck anything that gets him off. He

never told us he was bisexual until one of the brothers caught him with his dick in a guy's mouth one time while we were on a run.

"SUEDE." Batch comes barrelling into the room, screaming the Prez's name. His eyes scan the room, looking for him. Once their gazes connect, Batch is marching across the room and leans in, speaking into the Prez's ear.

I sit and watch as Batch explains whatever the hell is going on, Prez's face getting redder and redder as Batch keeps talking.

"CHURCH. NOW," Suede bellows to the room. "All non-members get the fuck out." He marches down the dark hallway towards the big room where we hold church, or club meetings to non-MC-know-it-alls. One of the newer prospects stands outside the room with two boxes; one for our mobile phones and the other for our weapons. Neither are allowed in church.

I walk into the room and most of the boys are here already. I take my seat to the left of Prez, dropping into the leather chair, and wait for Prez to start explaining what the fuck is going on. He bangs the gavel and rubs his hands over his face.

"We have trouble, boys. One of the girls from Silk was attacked last night as she was walking from her car to her flat."

Silk is one the businesses owned by the club. We own a community centre, where we rent time slots out for whatever the community needs. Then we have Silk, which is our strip club. We own a repair shop—Rider Repairs—and we also have boys working for Graves Construction, which is actually owned by Batch.

"What the fuck?" EC growls. The room is filled with, "How the fuck did that happen?" and "Do we know who did it?".

"Quiet down, for fucks sake, and I will explain."

"Who was hurt?" Bull's gruff question comes from across the table.

"Sienna," Batch answers.

"*Fuck.*" The boys mutter curses around the table. Sienna is one of the nicest girls you will ever meet, sweet as fuck. She dances to help pay for her ailing father's care home. The club offered to pay, but she refused. She's proud as fuck.

"So, do we know who did this, and why?"

"I don't care about the fucking why. I want to know *who* the hell did this," Suede raves. "These girls don't deserve this shit."

"Maybe Asia; she's a bitch on a good day." EC cackles. We all chuckle with him, because he's saying the truth. Asia is one mean bitch. She thinks she's the dog's dinner, bossing the other girls around. Bull's old lady, Alesha, runs Silk, and she has threatened to beat the shit out of Asia a few times.

We would get rid of her but, fuck me, the girl can dance. The men love her. Her and Eva have actually come to brawls over customers. Eva is the only dancer to stand up to her.

"Sienna said three men were waiting for her. One was in a suit and told her she should come and work for him. When she refused, his two goons beat the fuck out of her. She can't dance for a few weeks; her ribs are broken, and she has two cracking black eyes," Batch tells us.

"The girls will cover for her. We could bring in a new girl or two. I've been wanting to add some for a while now. Do you lads know of anyone who will dance?"

Suede looks around the room, waiting for a reply. And the usual fuckhead speaks.

"I know a few girls who might be looking for a job. Let me have a word with them and get back to you," EC announces. He always has his fingers in some pie or other. Or pussy or arse for that matter.

"Great, let me know." His look turns serious and I have a feeling I know what the old goat is going to say. "Ace, the funeral all sorted?" I nod. "Okay, we're here for you, brother. Anything you need, you let us know. The old ladies, too."

"How's Ana?" Bull pipes in. I swing my gaze to meet his concerned one. He cares for Ana just like the rest of the boys, but he and his old lady took a special liking to both Ana and Zarah.

"She's fine. Quiet, but that's the norm I would imagine. I know she's thinking of her parents with all this shit happening. She's still fussing over Z, like a mother hen, but that's my girl for you. I know all your women offered to help sort the food out for the wake, but Ana needs this. She needs to be busy—she told me."

"We're here for her, too, and for Z. Your brother coming?"

"Yeah, he messaged yesterday."

"Good, it will be good for him to be there with you. I think you both need this." I nod.

"Okay. Court, pop over to Silk and see how things are over there. Batch, you find out how Sienna is. Anything else?" Suede looks around the table, no one saying anything. He bangs the gavel down and speaks. "Okay, you ugly fuckers, you're all on cleaning duty today, except for those who I've given a job to do. I want this room perfect for Nancy's send off. She was like a mother to most of you, and I know how much you all loved and respected her." A lug-nut-sized ball of emotion clogs my throat.

All the boys nod to me when they leave the room. A few slap my back, offering their support and sympathy. My mother has well and fucking truly left her mark on the boys of the club—fuck, even some of the girls. Most of them respected my mum, but some not so much. That was because my darling mother caught me getting a blowjob from one of the girls, and she wasn't fazed. She just muttered, "When you're done playing with the trollop, please bleach your dick and come and help me move tables." From that day on, a few of the girls hated my mum, but they kept their thoughts to themselves.

"Ace." My name drags me from a past thought of my mum, and I look towards Suede and Dyson. They both stare at me with concerned faces, but they don't need to. I'm fucking fine—well, as fine as a man can be after losing the main woman in his life.

"Huh?"

"You need anything?" Dyson asks. I shake my head.

"Brother, you look wrecked. You been sleeping?" Pres asks.

"Some," I mutter, while walking out the room. "I need to see my woman."

"Is she yours, brother?" Suede speaks from behind me, and I spin around to look at him. My scowl makes him smirk at me.

"You know she is." My eyes bounce between father and son. Their smirks match each other's, just like their eyes.

"Does she know this? Ana keeps you at a distance, brother," Dyson tells us. But it's something I already know.

No one knows Ana's past, but I intend to find out. The boys never push her for more info, because one time they did, she freaked out and didn't come into work for two days, and Zarah went all mama bear on everyone. That woman is not scared of the club. She unleashed her inner bitch on us for hurting her sister.

"She knows, but that doesn't mean she's going to let him push her around and make demands." Suede laughs, making Dyson laugh too.

"Fuckers. Fuck off. She will be mine." I storm out of the club-house with Dyson's words at my back.

"Let me know how that works out for you, brother."

"PISS OFF," I bark back, and hear them laughing at my response.

They can all fuck off. *She will be mine.*

I sling my leg over my bike and start her up, then make my way to my woman. The cafe is always busy this time of day, but I need to speak to her.

The ride to the cafe doesn't take me long. I weave in and out of the cars that drive like Miss Daisy on a Sunday morning. I park my bike just down a bit from the cafe and walk the short distance. I see Tina and Clover walking towards me, dressed like they always are; like they enjoy the attention of the men in town.

"Ace, baby, I was hoping to see you at the clubhouse, but now that you're here, let's go for a ride. I could use a stress reliever." Clover closes the gap between us and wraps her arms around my neck, and I don't react quick enough to stop her.

A loud intake of breath catches our attention, and a smirk appears on Clover's face as she looks over her shoulder. There, I see Ana, looking every bit hurt. She quickly spins around and walks back into the cafe, leaving the dirty cups on the outside tables.

"Fuck," I grind out and push Clover away from me. She fake pouts but she knows what she has done.

"What the fuck? Why would you do that? No, wait, don't bother answering that. Fuck off out of my sight before I permanently ban you from the clubhouse." I'm fucking fuming with Clover right now. She reaches for me again, and I step back. She needs to fucking clue in; I don't want her skanky arse.

"Oh, come on, Ace. You know I can do you better than any other woman, especially better than a fucking Disney Princess wannabe like Ana-fucking-Dawkins. You need a woman who can handle you, Ace, and I can do that, babe. You know I can." I scoff at her words.

"You have no fucking clue what Ana can handle. You know she's my woman, so why the fuck would you touch me? You were good for a quick lay, Clo, some place to get my dick wet until I could claim Ana. But you weren't, and never will be, more—to me or the brothers in the club. Now fuck off before I change my mind." I don't stay around for her reply. I walk into the cafe in search of my woman.

The chatter from the customers fills the room as I walk in, then fades as I head straight out to the back because I can't see my woman. Zarah throws daggers at me with her eyes when I walk past, but I just smirk at her, making her huff out an angry breath.

I push through the door-curtain-thing that's supposed to help keep flies and insects out of the kitchen and find Tarina cooking away. Before I can speak, she points to the back door, which leads out to the back garden of the cafe. The building used to be a large house until the previous owner turned it into a café. Mum bought it a few years later.

I push the door open and see Ana sitting on the garden bench. She's looking down and playing with the buttons that run down the front of her green summer dress. Her long reddish-brown hair is like a curtain around her, shielding me from seeing her beautiful face. I walk closer and take a seat next to her. She doesn't flinch or react in any way, which makes me believe she feels me when I'm close to her, just like I feel when she's close to me.

"Babe, it's not what you think." Her head snaps in my direction. I can see the fury in her eyes, and it makes my cock jerk with happiness. I fucking love riling her up.

"That's what you're leading with? That's what you have to say when a club whore throws herself at you? God, Ace. *This* is why we won't ever work. I hated seeing that. I can't let my heart see that all the time." She bites her lip and turns away from me.

"Baby, it won't always be like that. Most of the girls stay away from me now. Clover thinks she has a claim on me, but I've put her straight more than once. When I officially claim you in the eyes of the club, and you wear my patch and my brand, no one will fuck with you. Not that they do now, because they know their balls are at stake if they even get any impure thoughts of you in their head." She giggles and brings her gaze back to me.

"Patch and brand?" She arches a perfect brow at me, and I smirk back.

"Yep. You are mine, Ana. I've told you this. No more fucking waiting. After tomorrow, I'm claiming you as my old lady in the eyes of the club, and you know what that means." I inch closer, so our lips are almost touching. Her warm breath slides over my lips and beard, making my dick jerk in my jeans again.

"What, Ace?" Her voice comes out in a breathy way, her body responding to how close mine is to hers.

"It means I can take you to bed and fuck you in ways you have never been fucked before. The whole fucking club will know that you are mine, now and for always."

Her breath catches, and her face turns beet red. I laugh and leave her sitting there on the bench. The laugh catches me off guard. It's the first time I've laughed like this in weeks—since Mum started to go downhill.

Now Ana knows where we stand, I now need to get my head around the fact I have to say my final goodbye to my mum.

Ana

Zarah and I closed up the cafe and decided to have a Chinese after work. We bought a bottle of wine to share, but she can only have one glass as she's still on painkillers for the injuries she's still healing from.

I had beef and broccoli with rice, and Zarah had special Chow Mein and rice. We put *Shadowhunters* on. We can binge watch tonight as we've missed three or four weeks of episodes.

"I can do with a Malec sandwich right now." We giggle as we watch a kissing scene between the characters Alec and Magnus. I take a sip of my wine and watch Jace come on the screen.

"Now that is a man I wouldn't kick out of my bed." I nod in the direction of the TV.

"Oh, hell yes. Have you seen his eyes?" Zarah gets a dreamy look in her eyes and I laugh at the look on my sister's face. I snort and choke on the wine that goes up my nose, and we burst into a fit of giggles, until Zarah sucks in a big breath when her laughter makes her ribs hurt.

"Bollocks, that hurt." I wince, and the sadness takes over again. The fear of losing Zarah a few weeks back... and then we lost Nancy. Sometimes I think I'm not destined to have absolute happiness in my life. Losing our parents was the catalyst of the fear that I will lose everyone I love.

Zarah was the only person I cared about until we moved here. Then I had Nancy and the boys. And Ace. The MC seem to have wormed their way into my heart without direct contact with it. They are sweet and kind, and fiercely loyal to the club and people who are close to them. They don't trust many, but those they do mean a lot to the club.

"Sooooo, what's up with you and Mr. McGowan?" My sister's voice drags me back to the here and now. I look at her and see her wiggling her eyebrows at me, and I laugh at her. Zarah has always been the funny one of us. The one that doesn't take life too seriously unless she has to.

"You are ridiculous, sis," I tell her. She chuckles and takes a sip of her drink.

"Maybe, but I still want the details. So come on, I need to know." I shake my head at her and sink down into the sofa more, wishing I could get Ace out of my head for just one second. I stare at the TV, unable to look at my sister's face when I tell her what Ace told me. Zarah as always been Team Ace; she thinks he will be good for me. That he will bring back the baby sister she once had, not the shell of a woman I am now.

"He told me that, after the funeral, he's claiming me in front of the club. That I—"

"Hold up. Claiming you in front of the club? I thought he'd pretty much already done that; it's why none of the boys touch you and you have the club's protection."

What she says is right; most people think Ace claimed me long ago but I was playing hard to get. But in true fact, no claiming was ever done. He told people I was off limits to everyone in the club, but also under the club's protection. I was also told by Nancy that Ace hasn't touched another woman since just after I turned up here and started working for her.

"I know. I think this claim is official as I have to wear his patch and have his brand tattooed on me." Zarah busts out laughing again. She clutches her ribs, holding them in place while she laughs at me.

"You. Tattoo..." she pants out between breaths. "Oh my lord, that is waaaay too funny. Does he really think you will have a tattoo?" I nod.

"Yeah, he told me I had to have his brand on me. I hate needles. Plus, am I ready to be claimed by him?" I shudder at the thought of being tattooed, but also the thought of being owned by someone.

I remember going with Zarah when she had her first tattoo. I almost fainted when I saw the needle. Zarah didn't flinch, but I was gagging and had to leave the room.

"Oh, now that will be fun. I'm so coming with you when you have it done." I shake my head, panic setting in. I can't have a tattoo. Nope, not happening.

"Nope," I say, and get up from the sofa and walk into the kitchen. "I can't have a tattoo. You know how I react to them. That's why I had to refuse the depo shot." My nurse had suggested I have the pill injection, and I had almost fainted when she was talking about it. Now I'm on the plain old pill—that I take without fail despite not needing them because I'm not sleeping with anyone.

Ace has let it be known he wants me to be his old lady many times, and it scares the crap out of me. However, things have changed, so maybe it is worth a shot.

Ace's face flashes in my head—and the words he told me; the things he wants to do to me. My body flushes and I stick my head in the fridge to cool my burning face down.

"What the bloody hell are you doing?" Zarah asks with humour in her voice. I spin around and squeak.

"Nothing?" I answer.

"Is that an answer or a question, baby sis?" I shrug. I turn back to the fridge and catch sight of the two cakes I have in there ready for Nancy's wake tomorrow. Tears fill my eyes and I lift my hand to my mouth to silence the sob threatening to break free. I'm going to miss her so bloody much. She was like a mum to Zarah and me.

Arms wrap around me from behind. I feel my sister press her face into my back, holding me together.

"You need to let it out, Ana. It isn't good for you to suppress the grief; it will cause you more mental pain." I shake my head and try with everything I have to drop the tears. "Do it, Ana, or I'll phone Ace to come here and deal with you."

"You wouldn't?" I snap at her and pull free. By the look on her face, I know she will.

"I bloody well will. You can't keep holding things in."

"Watch me. I don't have time to sit around and cry all bloody day, Z."

"Did I say you had to cry twenty-four-seven? No, I bloody well didn't. All I said was you have to let your emotions out. They will eat you alive. Now come here and cry on your big sister's shoulders; I can take it," she jokes, but I know she means everything she's saying.

"I love you, Z-Bug."

"I love you, too, Smallie." We giggle and take our fresh drinks back into the living room. "Now let's eat our weight in ice cream and watch hot blokes on the TV." I nod and get everything we need.

Zarah always knows how to get me out of my head and is the voice of reason sometimes, but other times I am so far buried in my head no one can get me out. It has been just us two for so long that I've gotten used to the idea of us growing old together with our many cats.

We sit and watch more shows on Netflix until Zarah remembers she bought the new Fifty Shades film, so we sit and watch—and drool—over Christian Grey, aka Jamie Dornan.

My phone buzzes on the coffee table, so I lean forward to pick it up. I smile when I see Ace's name on the screen, but then it fades. I can't imagine what he's feeling right now. He's saying his final goodbye to his mother tomorrow. I know that feeling all too well. The loss never goes away. I swipe the phone open and read the text.

Ace: Hey, baby. You okay?

Me: I'm okay. You?

Ace: Chilling at Mum's. The house feels empty.

My heart aches for him. Even after all these years, the pain of saying goodbye to my parents is still there. I don't think it ever goes away. That's the reason I can't listen to the band 'Wet Wet Wet'; they were my mum's favourite band.

Me: I can imagine. I have everything ready for tomorrow.

Ace: Good. I need you to take my mind of this heavy shit, babe. I'm going fucking crazy.

Ace doesn't normally show emotion when around the boys, so I'm surprised he's telling me this.

Me: What do you want to talk about?

Ace: You. Me. Us. Me making you mine. In. Every. Way.

I swallow hard, and my core clenches.

Me: Ace, all this talk of you claiming me... it scares the hell out of me. You scare me.

Ace: I would never hurt you, babe; you know that. Fuck, we've been through this shit before.

I glance over at Zarah, who is giving me a concerned look. I shake my head at her. She must know it's Ace who's texting because she nods in acknowledgement and turns to look at the TV. The scene on the TV makes my body heat up. God, I bet Ace would be amazing in bed. He looks like a man who's had plenty of experience and knows what he's doing. My phone vibrates in my hand, startling me from my thoughts.

Ace: Answer me, Ana. Tell me you know I would never hurt you.

Me: I know you won't. But my heart is another matter, honey.

Oh shit, that just slipped out and my finger clicked send before I could delete that 'honey' part. I bite my lips and watch as the three little dots appear as Ace writes his reply. But it doesn't come—the dots vanish. I look out the window next to the couch and see people sweeping past, walking their dog. I wonder if me and Ace will ever have a dog. *Whoa, where did that come from?*

My phone vibrates in my hand, but it isn't a text coming through. No, Ace's face lights up the screen, which means he's calling me. Oh no.

"I need to take this," I tell Zarah, and jump up and run out to the garden. The weather is a little chilly but nothing too bad.

"Hello?"

"I like that." Ace's voice comes through the phone and wraps around my body, making all kinds of emotions come to the surface. I know what he's talking about, but I ask anyway.

"Like what?" I sit down on the wooden bench.

"You calling me 'honey'. It means I'm getting somewhere with you. You care for me," he states matter of fact.

"Of course I care for you, Ace. We're friends." I cringe at the word *friends*. We're more than friends and we both know it, but my damned head is making me second guess everything.

"Friends? I don't want to be just your friend, Ana. I want to be your fucking everything. Can't you see that? Fuck me, you're turning me into some teenage girl here."

"God, Ace." I whisper his name as the lump in my throat grows. I cough and clear it to speak to him.

"You could never pull off the teenage girl look, even if you tried. You're too manly and handsome for that."

"You think I'm handsome?"

"Don't fish, Ace McGowan. You know the ladies love you." It's true; he always has desperate women fawning over him. I've seen plenty. But come to think of it, what I haven't seen is him actually do anything with them. They fuss over him but nothing else. Have I made us waste so much time because my head made up things to keep me from getting my heart hurt?

"I do know. But there's only one lady I want in my bed, panting out my name." He chuckles through the phone.

"Always with the sex talk, huh, Ace."

"Always, babe. Tomorrow, after the... the funeral, I want you to come home with me. Stay the night with me. No questions, no ifs, buts or maybes. *No* more waiting. I want to take you so fucking hard everyone will know who you belong to. I—"

"I don't belong to anyone, Ace," I snap, my voice rising in volume.

"But you already do, baby. You're the Unforgiven Rider's Sergeant-at-Arms' old lady. Everyone knows that, except you. You need to let that sink in. You have one more day, babe, then you're mine."

"I can't get a tattoo, Ace," I blurt out, then cover my mouth with my hand. Ace's laughter comes through the speaker, making my stomach knot. His laugh is sexy, deep, throaty and like velvet.

"So you're accepting that you're my old lady; you just don't want the tattoo brand."

"Damn it, Ace. I hate needles," I confess to him.

"Again, you're saying you belong to me; you just don't want the ink." I need to end this conversation before I open my mouth and spew more words, letting him get what he wants.

"It's late, Ace, and we both need sleep. Tomorrow is a big, emotional day. I'll see you in the morning." He sighs and my heart aches for him. I want to hold him and take his pain away. My head and heart need to be on the same page when it comes to Ace.

"Fine. But I'll send a prospect to pick you and Zarah up in the morning and bring you to the clubhouse. I I want you on my bike when we go to the cemetery." I don't want to argue with him tonight. He's going through a tough time, one I know all too well about. Losing a parent is never easy, no matter how old you are.

"Can they pick us up at the cafe? I need to make sure the food is ready to take to the clubhouse."

"Okay, babe." His voice seems sadder now that I've brought up the funeral. "I have two prospects transferring the food from the cafe to the clubhouse while we say... goodbye to Mum." The emotion that comes through the phone forces my own to surface.

"I wish I could hold you right now, Ace," I mutter, not quite sure he heard me.

"Me, too, babe. Do you think Zarah would care if I popped around?" I suck in a breath at his question. I don't think he heard me, but to be honest, I could do with seeing him and touching him. Damn, my head needs to catch up with my heart and body.

"She'll be fine with it. She's Team Ace," I partially joke. But what I said is true. She is rooting for Ace and me to be together, like she said earlier.

"On my way." He hangs up, not waiting for my reply. I jump off the bench and run into the house.

"Shit, Ace is coming over. Clean up while I sort my room." I run around like a headless chicken but stop dead in my tracks when I see Zarah gawking at me. "What?"

"Ace is coming here? Now?" I nod, and snap back into running back to my room, yelling my response to my sister.

"He is so fucking sad, Z. Nothing will happen; he just needs company."

"He has plenty of that at the clubhouse." Her words stop my actions of picking clothes up from the floor and throwing them into the laundry basket.

"Bitch. Why did you have to say that?"

"Proving a point: that you want Ace all to yourself." Okay, she does have a point there.

"Oh, shut it and clean, woman."

Not ten minutes later, Ace is knocking on the door. I fast-walk over and pull the door open for him. He looks ragged; dark circles under his eyes, hair looking greasy, like he's run his hand through it a million times today. My heart aches at the sight.

"Come on." I take his hand and lead him to my bedroom. Zarah went to her room right before he got here. Each step closer to my room makes my heartrate speed up. I feel Ace's grip tighten on my hand, and I look around to face him. He offers me a small smile, which I return.

I push my bedroom door open and step aside for Ace to follow. I close the door behind him, nervous about what to do next, but Ace takes the first step. He removes his club cut and places it on the back of my desk chair, before removing his white t-shirt. It's Ace's signature outfit: dark jeans, white t-shirt and black biker boots.

I'm already in my jammers, but they're hidden under my dressing gown.

"Get in bed, babe." His voice is gruff, making me shiver. His lips quirk at the move. I untie the rope as I watch Ace finish undressing. I stand there, stunned, looking at the man before me. Tattoos cover both arms from wrist to shoulder, abs for days, and the special V. My mouth waters and my core clenches, but thoughts like this shouldn't be present tonight. Now is not a good time.

Ace climbs into the bed and settles on the left. Did he know I sleep on the right? I shake my head and look at his face. His eyes are fixed on me—more like my whole body. His eyes scan me from head to naked feet. I'm in white cotton shorts and matching camisole vest with lace over the breast area. I may not flash a load of skin in public, but I like to dress comfy but flirty in bed. It's my thing. Gary hated it.

"Damn, babe. Are you sure we can't have sex tonight?" he

asks, and reaches under the blanket to adjust his dick. I squeeze my thighs together, and Ace chuckles, seeing the effect he's having on me.

"Nope. No sex." I climb in and Ace immediately pulls me to him and wraps his arms around me. I sigh in content at the feel of them caging me close to him. I feel safe with Ace. I always have.

His breathing evens out, and I can tell he's slipping into sleep.

"Night, baby." His warm breath washes over my bare shoulder, making my skin pebble with goose bumps.

"Night, honey," I say, now knowing he likes that. His arms tighten briefly before we both fall into deep sleep.

Nine

Ace

I STARE AT THE WHITE CEILING, WAITING FOR ANA TO WAKE UP. I wish today was like any other day, but it isn't. It's the day I have dreaded most in my thirty-two-years. Today is the day I bury the woman who gave me life, who fed and clothed me, and who taught me how to be the man I am today.

My mum was probably my best friend, and I'm man enough to admit that. She was there when I needed her, even though I was a hellion growing up. She bought me my first bike—bought me my first pack of condoms when she caught me and Becca McGee kissing and being a little hands-on in the garden when we were fifteen. I chuckle as the memory of her face comes into my head.

Ana stirs next to me, and I look down at her. She's been my saving grace these past few weeks, even without knowing it. I've acted all tough biker on the outside, lashing out when I get angry, but inside I've been becoming more and more numb to the fact my mother passed away.

I risk stretching over to get my phone to check the time. I'm pretty sure Ana set an alarm but fuck if I know. I pick up the phone and see it's eight-ten a.m. We have plenty of time. Mum's funeral isn't until ten-thirty.

"Morning," comes the sweetest voice ever known to man. Her voice is full of sleep but holds a promise of sex in its huskiness.

"Morning, darlin'." I pull her tighter and grip her thigh, which is draped over mine. Her gasp makes me smile. I don't think she realised how she was lying.

"How you feeling, Ace?" She clears her throat of any sleep, and I'm slightly disappointed about that. Ana's sleepy voice is sexy as hell. I change our position so we're laying on our sides, face to face. Her eyes still hold some sleepiness to them, but blue in them are bright and showing her emotions. She's just as sad about today as I am. She thought the world of my mum.

"Don't know. Lost maybe." I lift my hand and slowly trace her jawline with my fingers. Her eyes close at the touch, making my heart swell with happiness in this time of darkness surrounding us.

"You aren't lost, honey. You're here with me and the club. No matter what happens, you are never alone. You know that." I nod and lean in and lay a gentle kiss on her lips. I don't deepen the kiss—even if the need to do so is raging inside of me. Now is not the time to claim her for the first time. When we fuck for the first time, it will take me all night to cover every inch of her perfect body.

"Always first and last," I say, before slipping out of bed. I hear her quick intake of breath and walk over to the chair to pick up my clothes. I pull them on and Ana watches me without saying anything. I sneak little glances at her and notice her cheeks are burning red as she sees me half naked, my cock almost breaking through the material of my boxers.

Once I've pulled my cut over my shoulders, I walk back to the bed. Ana is sitting up, holding the blanket close to her body, trying to hide from me. *Yeah, not going to happen.*

"Don't ever hide from me, babe. I want to see you. Always." I lean in for a kiss but pull back quickly, causing Ana to moan in frustration. I smirk at her. Her body tells me something completely different to her words.

"You'll have all of me soon enough, baby. I promise you that. Get ready, while I pop home and do the same. Then I'll come back so I can get us to the cafe. Solar and Jas will be there soon. Solar is riding beside me—behind Mum. Jasmine will be in the family car with you." She nods and climbs from the bed.

I ride home and take a quick shower, so I can get back to my girl. When I'm around her, the numbness fades. It doesn't suck me in.

I slowly slide my cut on over the crisp white shirt Ana got me. She bought the same for the boys too, because none of us had shirts to wear. My stomach clenches at the sight in the mirror. This is what I'll wear to say goodbye, for the final time I will see her.

I shake my head and take a deep breath, before leaving the room. Locking the door behind me, I walk over to my bike and mount up. The ride to the cafe is a short one, and before I know it, I can see people standing around. It's like a sea of people, there at that many here who have come to give Mum a good send off.

Ana walks over to me and takes my hand in hers. Solar and Jasmine are standing just up from the cafe. We walk over to them hand in hand, and that does something to my heart.

"Hey, guys," Ana says as we approach my brother and his woman.

"Hi," Jasmine replies, and the two women hug. I look at Solar and see him watching me.

"You okay?" he asks me while shaking my hand and patting me on the back.

"Yeah. I'll be glad when it's all over." I scrub my hand over my beard. I take a deep breath and Ana must see the struggle trying to break free.

"Ace, let's go and grab a coffee." I nod and point to where Mum's cafe is.

"Mum's cafe is just over there. I'd love for you to see it. We're gonna ride behind the funeral car from there."

"We can walk from here," Ana explains.

"Follow me, bro." Solar nods, and we watch as our women link arms and walk in front of us. We walk in silence, and then we're at the cafe.

"Come on in," I say, and slap my brother on the back. The place is packed with brothers and family of the club.

"Everyone," I bark over the noise. Everyone goes quiet, and my heart speeds up in my chest. I'm about to introduce my long-lost fucking brother my MC family. "I'd like to introduce my brother, Solar. He's from the Cornish Crusaders MC down in Cornwall. He'll be riding with me today." All my brothers climb to their feet and come over to greet my brother.

"Hey, I'm Dyson—VP."

"I'm EC." Each of the boys talk to Solar and Jasmine until it's time. My face drops for a split second, remembering why we're all here. The bottomless pit opens and threatens to suck me in. Ana comes to stand next to me and again takes my hand in hers.

"They're making their way to the church," I say to the room.

"Yeah, we should get going too." I pull Ana and hug her tight to me. Her smell invades my senses and memories of this morning come flooding back. She goes up on her tiptoes and whispers in my ear.

"Always." My breath gets caught in my lungs, but I hold myself firm. I nod and let my eyes do the talking. They hold hers for a moment, and she sees me. I nod again and kiss her forehead, before turning to Solar.

"I just wanted to show you this before we left." He follows me over to the wall of photos. He stares at the photo of us as newborn babies. I can feel the sadness seep from him, because I can feel the sadness creeping in too.

"Mum asked me to have this blown up and frame it here. She told me this was the one picture she always kept with her. She said that if I ever found you, to tell you her heart broke having to leave you, that she always loved you and hoped, one day, you could find it in your heart to forgive her." The emotions take over, and my chest feels like it's caving in with the weight of not having Mum around.

I clench my fist, trying to rein in my grief.

"I don't remember her. I don't remember what she looked like or anything." His eyes stay firmly on the photo of us.

"Here." I pull out the box of photos I have of Mum for him. His eyes flick over our mother in each photo. My heart literally aches for him, for not knowing such an amazing woman.

"Who is older?"

"That would be me, little brother. By a whole seven minutes." I chuckle. Talking to him seems easier than what it was when we first met. I just wish I'd had him all my life. Things would have been so fucking different when we were growing up. I know we would have had each other's backs.

Brothers in blood, stick together like mud, one of the old-timers used to say.

I check my phone for the time. My stomach gets heavy, knowing the time is closing in on our final goodbye. I clench my fists and take a deep breath.

"Come on, let's lock up. The car will be here any minute." The hair on the back of my neck stands on end as I see the funeral car carrying my mum's body coming around the corner. My eyes stay locked on the coffin in the back, even as the car comes to a stop. I can't stop staring.

Mary, from the funeral directors, climbs out of the car and stops by my brother and me.

"Ace, how are you?" Her voice is soft, perfect for her job.

"Not too bad. This is my brother—"

"Aiden." My brother introduces himself.

"Nice to meet you. I'm sorry for your loss. Once we get to the gate of the church, I'll climb out and walk in front of the car. You continue on your bikes and then follow the coffin inside the church," Mary explains to us. We both nod and climb onto our bikes. Brothers in blood and arms riding side by side for the first time... It's a fucking shame it took our mum dying to bring us together.

The ride to the church is uneventful. I see a few people stand on the side of the road, with their hands over their hearts. My mum has well and fucking truly left her mark on the town.

We pull up at the big steel gates leading to the church. We park our bikes and climb off. Our women walk towards us. I can see Ana has been crying again. Jasmine rubs her back soothingly.

"You ready?" I ask Solar as Jasmine comes to stand next to him. Ana slides her hand into mine, making my breath hitch. He nods, and we follow the coffin into the final resting place of the woman who gave us life.

Listening to Zarah talking about the type of woman my mum was, makes me want to throw up. The thought of never seeing her again... My chest feels like a ten-ton lorry is sitting on it. My fists clench and unclench as I try to bring my emotions under control.

A tiny, soft hand slides over my rough, tanned ones. My skin erupts in goose bumps as Ana takes my hand in hers and gives me a little squeeze.

After Zarah settles back down in her seat, Ana steps up to the altar to say a few words about Mum, and I know I can't follow up with my own. I'm drowning in emotion. I look at Aiden and see he's taking in every word she's saying, just like he did when Zarah spoke. I see regret pass over his face. Does he wish he looked for us sooner?

Once the funeral is over, everyone comes over to Aiden, Ana and me and gives us their condolences for Mum's passing. I hate it. I just want to get absolutely fucking hammered. I just want today to be over with.

After we get back to the clubhouse, Aiden explains to me about the wanker of a man who is our father. He tells me he died a while ago. I feel fuck all for the man. We talk about staying in touch—for fucks sake, we are blood brothers. Then I watch as they drive off.

I stand there for fuck knows how long, watching the clouds move across the sky. Mum always used to say to enjoy the little things. Most of the time, when she said that, it was when Ana was in the room. It was her way of telling me to enjoy Ana and all the little things she does, and to make sure I don't miss anything. Just like she missed to much of Aiden's life; she never got to meet her grandson and future grandkids.

"How you doing, brother?" Court asks as he steps up beside me.

"Fuck knows, man. I feel numb and empty, as girly as that sounds. But it's the fucking truth. I miss her, man." I swallow hard.

"Life is fucking shit, Ace. Nothing we can do about it but live it to the max. Don't regret anything, that's what I always say. You know that." I nod because he's saying the truth; he doesn't regret a fucking thing he does.

Court got his road name when he became the club's lawyer. Yep, Court is a fully-qualified lawyer. Not that he can practice law anymore.

He was defending some prick his company made him defend.

The guy was a piece of work, and one day he said the wrong thing in the courtroom. Our Court decked him, laid the fucker out, so he got fired and then later disbarred. He served eighteen-months for assault. He joined the club as soon as he came out and hasn't looked back.

"Go inside and down a few shots, get fucking smashed, man. You deserve it. Nancy was a badarse lady, and she will be missed." With them parting words, he walks back into the clubhouse.

His words sink in and I know he's right. Now is the time to regret nothing. Now is the time to remember all the little things and *always* get what's mine.

Ana

I PICK UP THE DIRTY GLASSES AND CARRY THEM INTO THE KITCHEN for the girls to clean and get back out to the bar. The boys are drinking up a storm. Some of the club girls weren't happy they had to help, but Suede put his foot down and made them do it.

Clover keeps glaring at me, but I try my best to ignore her. She's the main girl here who wants to sink her claws into Ace. Bile threatens to rise with the thoughts of them being together, because I know Ace has slept with her before. He's probably slept with all the club girls here. I force the gut-wrenching thoughts out of my head and carry on cleaning up.

I walk back out into the bar, carrying a tray of already clean glasses. I smile at Suede and Lola as I pass. They are amazing together. Lola once told me they had a difficult time getting together due to her strict parents, but her love for Suede won in the end. I hear a bark of laughter and turn to see some of the boys sitting around one of the tables, drinks in hand, laughing and talking about Lord knows what.

My gaze scans the room and I see Ace sitting with Batch and Dyson. He must sense me looking at him because his head lifts and his eyes meets mine. The smile that crosses his face makes my breath catch in my throat. A look of longing and wickedness fills his gaze.

I smile back at him and carry on my walk towards the bar. I place the full tray on top of the bar and go about putting them away. Once that's done I walk back to the kitchen. I'm almost there when I'm pushed against the wall, but not forcefully. The scent of leather, smoke and oil surrounds me.

"Do you know how much I want you?" Ace's husky voice floats into my ear. His warm breath coats the bare skin on my neck.

"I do," I whisper back. His hands trail up my sides, over my ribs, but stop before touching my breasts. One hand stays below my left breast while the other slides down to my hip. Ace grips the hem of my black dress and starts to pull it up. Panic rises inside me as anyone can walk down the hallway and catch us.

I reach down and stop his movements.

"What?" he asks.

"You need to stop. It's not the place, honey."

"Baby, it's *always* the place when me and you are concerned."

"Ace, stop. Later," I reply.

"Promise." I nod, no words forming as his left hand moves to cup my breast.

"Ace."

"Promise me, baby. Promise me I get to finally touch you later. That I get to taste you like I know we both want."

My heart rate spikes and my palms start to sweat—and I am pretty sure he can feel that as my hand is still resting on top of his. His beard scratches my neck as he leans in to kiss the bare skin. Goose bumps cover my body at the contact.

"I promise, Ace." My voice isn't quite sounding like me. He leans in more, scraping his teeth over the tendon in my neck. I moan, making Ace growl in reply. His erection is pressing into my backside, making my core throb in delight and want.

"Good, baby. Don't make me come hunting for you."

"I won't. I'll be here. *Always.*"

"Always, baby. Always. Now go and help the other old ladies. I'll catch you later." He walks away, leaving me to shiver and missing his contact. I rest my head on the cool wall, willing my body to calm down. I smile to myself, thinking about all the wicked things he will be doing to me later.

There's no point in trying to stop this from happening anymore. Ace always gets what he wants, and it's evident he wants me. Little Ana Dawkins.

"He'll get bored you know." The voice that grates on my nerves comes from my left. I straighten up and turn to face Clover.

"Leave me alone, Clover." She laughs in my face, making my back go rod straight.

"You can never handle a man like Ace. He likes... well, let's say certain things done to him during sex. Things I know a bratty little girl like you would never do. Ace don't do vanilla, bitch. So I suggest you walk the fuck away." Her voice gets louder as she baffles on.

"What happens with me and Ace is none of your concern, so I suggest *you* walk away."

"Don't you see that he only ever wanted you because you were a challenge for him? You were there at the cafe and he saw you as a challenge." Her words are like a barb to the heart. It hurts like hell. Surely she can't be correct?

"Now that Nancy is dead, he can sell the cafe and you will be a long forgotten memory of pussy that wouldn't give it up to him." I gasp at her vile words.

"SHUT UP! You don't get to talk about Nancy or the cafe to me. Now back the fuck off." My temper is rising, and I swear to God I will knock this chick out if she continues to mouth off. I hate confrontation, but sometimes my inner bitch comes out to play.

"Just leave, Ana, then Ace can go back to shagging me on a

regular basis and I can suck his cock, just like he likes it. Just like I did the other night." I gag and cover my mouth with my hand. Bile almost wins its race in leaving my stomach. Clover smirks at me because she knows she's hurt me.

"What the fuck is this?" Lola questions, while walking down the hallway.

"Nothing, Lola. Just telling Ana how things are around here." I lock eyes with Lola and hers narrow on me. I drop my hand and step around them both. I walk through the main room and make a beeline for the front door. I need air.

"Ana." I ignore the person calling my name and push through the door.

"Stop, now," another voice comes.

"Smallie?" Zarah's voice makes my steps falter. I finally stop over by the picnic bench and take a seat. I close my eyes and take a few deep breaths, hoping it will stop the need to vomit over the table.

I watch as Zarah's shadow looms over me before she takes a seat opposite me. We sit in silence for a few moments, neither of us saying anything. The stillness is peaceful, yet it doesn't calm my raging heart and the thoughts of *him* with *her*.

I knew he had been with other girls before, but I thought that since he was after me, he wouldn't be with the club girls. Clearly, I was wrong about him.

"Smallie, talk to me." Z's voice breaks through the visions in my head.

"I thought he was different. Don't get me wrong, I know what goes on in the club, but the way Ace is with me... I just thought he was different. I guess not."

"Talk to him, hun. You know what these skanks are like. They like stirring shit." Her hand covers mine, offering me a gentle squeeze.

"I don't know," I whisper.

"I know you like him—if not more." I go to speak but she lifts her hand to stop me. "Stop hiding it. You feel for him; you know you do. Now pull your big girl knickers up and go in there and claim your man." She wiggles her eyebrows at me, making me giggle. She looks at me with such love and adoration in her eyes that I can't find it in me to let her down. She's right: I do deserve happiness, and if that happiness is in the form of Ace McGowan, the Unforgiven Riders' Sergeant-at-Arms, then so be it.

"He can hurt me, Z," I mutter.

"And he may not. You can't keep thinking every man will hurt you. We've been over this before. Give it a try."

I think over her words, letting them sink in good and proper.

"He likes the attention he gets from the club girls, and I can't compete with them, Zarah. He's been free to sleep with anyone and everyone for years. He isn't going to change overnight, and that scares the hell out of me." I pull the black hair tie from my wrist and haphazardly tie my hair back. I know little tendrils of hair will come loose, but for now it will have to do.

"You are bloody beautiful, and no one will tell you any different. Ace likes you for you, Ana, not because he thinks you'll give a good blowjob and are a firecracker in bed. He sees beyond that with you."

"And thank you for the mental image of Ace in bed with many other women." Zarah sighs and looks away. My chest tightens at the disappointment on her face. I have always suffered with images issues—thanks to the wanker who no longer shall be named.

I need to do this for me, and for Zarah. I need to show her I'm ready to move on, that I'm ready to take back my life and be Ana Dawkins. The girl who once used to be quick-witted and feisty, just like her big sister.

"I'm gonna do it." I stand up with my determination, but forget that I'm sitting on a picnic bench. My legs jam against the seat, and I lose my balance and go flying backwards onto the grass.

"Small—" But her laughter cuts off her words. I lay there staring up at the clear blue sky, laughing my arse off. Zarah's laughter fills the air above me. Bitch.

Once we stop laughing, I lean up on my elbows and look at my sister. She's wiping tears from her eyes, and her smile's filling her once again unmarked face.

"A little help here, big sis." She takes a deep breath before coming around to my side and lifting me to my feet.

"Classy, Miss Dawkins. Classy as fuck." We laugh again, and I link arms with her as we walk back into the clubhouse.

Zarah pushes through the door, and I follow. Music is still playing loudly through the speakers. The brothers are all mulling around, if in different parts of the room. I see Lola sitting next to Suede in the corner. His face buried in her neck, making her giggle and slap his chest. Her eyes connect with mine, and she offers me a small nod. She knows what I'm about to do.

I look around the room and see Ace standing by the bar with Dyson and Court. Double D is standing way too close for my liking, but she's about to be put in her place. Hopefully.

"You got this," Zarah whispers in my ear before walking off to sit with EC and some of the other boys. They all take care of Zarah. I think Ace has threatened them a few times to keep their hands off her.

I take slow steps towards the bar. Court watches me from the corner of his eye but doesn't say anything. As I get closer, Dyson spots me and offers me a short nod, but he never stops talking. Double D sees the action and looks over her shoulder at me, before stepping closer to Ace. He pulls away, but it's not enough and she runs her hand up his chest. My fists curl into balls, ready to punch her if needed. I am not a violent person, but these club girls bring the nasty side out in me.

"Ana," Dyson says in greeting. Ace's head snaps in my direction, but he doesn't say anything. I raise an eyebrow at him and my gaze moves from his to Double D's hand, and then back to his eyes, showing him I'm not happy. She got her name when she joined the club—as you can guess, she loves two dicks in her at once.

"When will you ever learn, Ana? You can't handle the men in this club."

I don't back down or cower from her words. I need to stand up to these so-called women.

"I'm not after any other man in the club..." Now it's Ace's turn to raise an eyebrow at me. "Except for the man you're touching. So do us all a favour and live up to your name and piss off." I rest my hands on my hips. Dyson and Court fail to stop their laughter breaking free. Ace looks smugly at me. He likes the idea of me fighting with other girls over him. I wink at him and he tries to move away from the skank, but she steps with him.

"Any time now would be good for me," I add. She scowls at me and takes a step closer.

Ace

I can't take my eyes off my girl as she faces-off with Double D. It's sexy as fuck to see how she's standing up to a club girl over me. Me; the man she said she could never be with.

"Any time now would be good for me," Ana tells Double D.

"What are you going to do, Ana Banana?" I see the fire ignite in my girl's eyes. She fucking hates being called that. Ana has a wired hatred for bananas. The word, the smell, the actual fruit.

I step closer to Ana and wrap my arm around her waist. Her heat soaks into my side.

"I suggest you find another man to keep you company from now on, Margret." Ana uses Double D's birth name, and it sends her into a fit of rage. She hates her birth name as much as Ana hates the nickname.

"Shut the fuck up, you little cunt."

"Double D, watch your mouth," I tell her with a growl. She smirks at me and my stomach drops with dread about what will come out of her mouth next.

"You didn't mind my mouth the other day. Or the time before that. Or—"

"SHUT UP," I yell, making the room go silent, and both

women jump. Ana steps away from me, looking like she's ready to cry. My heart cracks at that single look.

"Ana, baby—"

"Don't." She puts her hand up, motioning me to stop talking. "God, how stupid was I to think you were different."

"She's lying."

"Really, Ace, that's what you're going with?"

"It was before things got heated between us."

"But you've been actively pursuing me for over a year, Ace. So while I was thinking with my head and my heart, you were thinking with your dick. Nice to know I mean that much to you."

"You mean *everything* to me, babe. You know that." I step closer to her, hooking my hand around her neck, keeping her from moving away from me. "Every-fucking-thing." I lean in and lay a kiss on her lips. It's not a claiming kiss, but it's a kiss full of promise.

"Ace, I—" I cut her off and spin her around so her back is to my front. I whistle loudly, getting everyone's attention.

"Listen up, fuckers. See this woman here?" I tighten my grip on Ana's waist. "You will show her the respect you show me and the club. Ana is my old lady, officially as of today. Anyone, and I mean any fucker, who disrespects her, is showing a direct insult to me. You will be kicked out of the club—unless you wear a patch, and then you get a fucking beating from me."

"And me," Dyson adds.

"Me too," Suede shouts from his seat in the corner. I look around the room and see the boys nod at me.

"Are you fucking serious? Her—when you can have any woman you want?" DD says, disgust dripping from her voice.

I spin around so fast Ana almost trips over. I right her body and push her in Dyson's direction slightly.

"Know your fucking place, bitch," I growl, and step closer. "You are here to be fucked by the brothers who want to get their dicks wet, and that's all. Your opinion is not needed, nor fucking wanted. You get me?"

"But *her*..." Double D points at Ana. "Come on, Ace. Really? You can do so much better."

Fuck me, she never listens.

"Clearly he can do better, because he came to me after being with all you club girls. If the other boys want to sleep with you, they can, but from now on, stay the hell away from Ace." Fuck me, my girl just claimed me back. In a split second, Double D flies at Ana. Her war cry could be heard miles away from how high-pitched it goes.

"YOU CUNT!" I watch in disbelief as Double D slams into Ana. They both go flying to the floor. Double D is on top of Ana, throwing slap after slap, but my girl is defending her face. I move to separate them, but Ana rolls and pins Double D to the floor. Now it's Ana's turn to take the lead.

Is it wrong my cock is hard as steel at the sight of my girl fighting?

Ana punches her in the face, over and over again. Who would have thought my girl had this much fire in her? Ana grabs a handful of bleach-blond hair and lifts Double D's head, before slamming it into the wooden floor.

Oh fuck, this could get nasty, real fucking quick.

I leap forward and pull Ana off, while Court pulls Double D to her feet. I keep my girl tight to my body, wiping her hair out of her eyes.

"Shh, baby, calm down. You can't act like this. You're an old lady now; you have to show restraint and act when the time is right." I take it that was the wrong thing to say. A feral growl comes from Ana, shocking even me. She pulls away from me, her hair hanging around her face, making her look even scarier.

"Show restraint? Is that what you want, *Ace*?" she growls out. "Are you fucking kidding me?" she screams at me. "Fuck you and your club whores. They're fucking welcome to you. I just claimed you, just like you claimed me, but it's totally okay for these cunts to throw themselves at you, and I have to stand by and watch. Not fucking likely. So as I said, they are FUCKING WELCOME TO YOU." Her fists are clenched. Even spit comes flying out of her mouth.

Holy fucking shit, she is angry.

I gaze around the room and see everyone watching the show. Prez and Lola are shaking their heads at me, showing their disappointment in me for not sticking up for my girl.

"Pack your shit and get the fuck out," Dyson barks at Double D. Fear fills her wide eyes, shocked she's being punished.

"Me? Why me? I've been here longer than her."

"Mouse is an old lady; you're a club whore. She takes priority over you any fucking day. You not only disrespected an old lady and her old man, but you laid a hand on her."

I stand there stock still, taking in the scene in front of me. I have never had two women come to physical fighting over me before, and to be completely fucking honest, it is a fucking turn on, but not for the reason some may think. Seeing Ana fight for me has my cock ready to come in my jeans.

"ANA." My girl's name being called snaps me out of my daze. My head turns to where Ana was just standing to find the spot empty. My eyes flicker over the room, and I see her running for the main door. Like fuck, woman.

I run after her, calling her name, but the little firecracker ignores me. I catch up to her in no time—bonus for being over six-feet-tall. I snatch her hand and pull her to a stop.

"Where the fuck are you going?" I snap at her.

"Home. Away from you. I'm done here."

"Like fuck you are," I bark back. I know Ana isn't scared of me, but she flinches a little at the loudness of my voice. I'm fucking pissed she thought she could just leave without us sorting this shit out. She tries to pull her hand from my grip, but I tighten my fingers along her slim wrist.

"Let me go, Ace."

"Not on your fucking life." I bend at the waist and slam my shoulder into her stomach, and heave her over my shoulder, fireman lift style. Her screams echo around the courtyard but I don't give a fuck. I stride back into the clubhouse. I ignore the cheers and keep up my pace. I nod to Dyson, and my brother can read what I want

He knows I want him to make sure Double D leaves and never fucking comes back. Dyson and me have always had this connection. We've known each other since we were four years old and started school together.

"Put me down, Ace McGowan, or you will regret it." I slap her arse, making her yelp.

"OW," she screams. I chuckle and slap her again. God, if my mum could see us now... She would be smiling at us. She always made it clear she wanted Ana and me together, well now she gets her wish. I am taking my woman. Now.

I push open my room door and not so gently toss Ana on the bed, before slamming and locking the door behind me. Ana stands and moves towards the door, which is behind me. I chuckle at her attempt.

"I want to leave," she mutters, anger still clearly evident in her voice.

"Tough shit. You aren't going anywhere. We're going settle this once and for all."

"Ace." This time her voice drops so low I can barely hear my name.

"You are mine. No more running, even when club girls get in the way." I hold my hand up when she goes to speak. "I fucked up out there. I get that. I should have said something to her, but, baby, you handled yourself pretty fucking well."

"Fuck off, Ace." She crosses her arms, making her tits push up, but I can't see them because she's still wearing the black dress she wore to Mum's funeral. Thinking of what's happened over the last few weeks makes me feel old. I feel tired but energized at the same time. My body is fucked up.

I know most people think I should be a quivering mess after burying my mum this morning, but everyone grieves differently. Nancy Harris would not want us to mourn her death. She would want us to celebrate her life. She told us plenty of times when we knew her time was close.

I step closer to Ana and she steps back. We keep doing this until her legs hit the side of the bed. She slumps down on the mattress, looking up at me with her big blue eyes. Eyes that show her emotions like a beacon in the night.

"We're together, baby, so we'll sort this shit out together. But I have one condition." I smirk at her. Confusion crosses her face.

"And what is that?"

"We talk naked. I want us bare to each other. That way there is no hiding." I don't wait for her response. I pull my cut off my shoulders and turn to lay it over the back of the chair in my room. My room is one of the bigger ones here at the clubhouse. I have an en suite and a small kitchenette, as well as my king-size bed, dressing table, wardrobe and a bedside table. Not much. I like things simple.

I turn back to Ana and start to unbutton the white shirt I wore for today. Ana sits there watching my every move, even when I drop the shirt and go for my belt. I toe off my boots and bend to pull off my socks. My jeans go next, dropping to the floor at my feet.

"Oh." Ana gasps, and I smirk at her response. It's the same one I get from all the girls. I am big—like fucking big. Long and thick as fuck.

"You like what you see, baby?"

"There's a lot to see," she compliments. My dick jerks from her stare. He wants her as much as I do. I wave my hand in the direction of her body and tell her to strip.

"Clothes off, babe." I can't stop my hand as it reaches for my dick. I need to add pressure to it because fuck me, we have had to deal with a shit load of blue balls around this woman. My hand and my dick have become very good friends lately.

Ana moves slowly, like she's waiting for me to change my mind about being naked. Well, that isn't going to happen. I watch as she lifts the hem of the dress and slides it up her body, before dropping it on the floor, leaving her in a black and cream, lace knicker and bra set.

Fuck me.

Her tits are perfectly firm. They look like they were made for sucking, biting and licking. My dick responds by jerking in her direction.

"Off." I motion to her underwear, and she does as she's told. "On the bed, babe." Thank fuck she listens. Ana climbs under the covers and I walk around to my side of the bed and join her.

"I don't get why we need to do this naked, Ace." Her voice is almost a whisper.

"I kinda lied, baby. We don't need to talk about fuck all; I've said all there is to say. I just wanted you naked and in my bed." I chuckle at the shocked look on her face.

I lift my hand and cup her breast. She shivers at the contact, making me smile. Her gaze stays locked on mine as I lower my head and take her nipple between my lips. God, her skin feels amazing. The nipple tightens as I run my tongue around it, shaping it.

"Oh hell," comes from her mouth in a breathy tone. I shift on the bed so I can play with the other nipple with my fingers. Her back arches off the bed as she moans my name. Her nipples are sensitive as fuck. Good to know. I suck hard on the bud and her body shivers again.

"You like your nipples being played with, babe?" She nods, keeping her eyes tightly closed. "Give me them eyes, baby. I want you to see who's going to make you come."

"Like I can forget that." Her answer makes my heart swell and my dick dribble. I leave her tits and make my way down her body. Ana's touch never seems to leave my skin. I love skin to skin contact with her. I've slyly touched her skin whenever the fuck I could just to feel the creaminess of her.

I reach her pussy and smile to myself when I see the thin line of hair, like a landing strip letting me know where she wants my mouth, or fingers, or dick. That landing strip if for 'Air Ace' *only.*

I bury my nose in her swollen pussy lips and take a deep breath, filling my lungs with her scent. I slide my hand around the small of her back and place the other on her flat stomach, holding her in place as I swipe my tongue over her pussy.

It's my turn to moan as her taste explodes across my tongue. I feast on her, making her moan my name in between pants.

I lick, suck and taste her like a starving man. I feel a hand on my mine—the one still resting on her stomach—and then one slides into my hair, holding me in place.

"Oh God, Ace. Right there," she pants out. Then she shocks the fuck out of me when she drags my hand up her body, over the centre of her chest, and rests it on her lips. I lift my gaze in time to see my girl open those perfect fucking lips and suck my fingers into her mouth.

Holy fucking shit.

Ana

THE GROAN THAT LEAVES ACE WHEN I SUCK HIS FINGERS INTO MY mouth makes my core flood with juices. He continues to feast on me, ensuring his tongue traces over every inch of my lower lips. I keep his hand in mine but rest it between my breasts. I can feel the tingle start, but it stops all too quickly. I snap my head up to stare down at Ace, finding him looking up at me.

"Fucking hell, baby. That was some sexy shit."

"Well get back to it; I was about to come." He smirks at me and does one long, firm lick of me, devouring me with his gaze as he does. I keep my eyes open, taking in his face buried between my legs.

His face comes into full view, and I can see the slight glistening of my arousal on his beard. I bite my lip and watch as he stalks up my body. He's like a hungry lion about to devour his prey—and I am that prey. God help me and my vagina.

I am so lost in the scene playing out in front of me—well, actually on top of me—that I don't register what's happening until Ace is lining up his dick at my entrance and slamming into me. Hard and deep.

I scream out his name as he growls mine. The sensation of being filled by this man is overwhelming.

"Oh God," I cry out.

"Not God, baby. Just Ace will do. Fuck, you feel so damn good, baby. Wet, warm… and un-fucking-believable." He buries his head into the nook of my neck, his beard scratching the overly sensitive skin.

"Waited too long for this. Never giving it up. Never. You are mine for-fucking-always, Ana." He growls out each word between hard thrusts. He shifts his body, and the new angle hits the spot inside me no man has ever reached. My back arches off the bed and I call out his name.

"ACE. God, that feels good." I wrap my legs around his trim hips, holding him tightly to me as he buries himself as deep as he can from this position. Our bodies move in sync, sweat covering our skin. I drag my nails over his back, marking him. An intense feeling slides over my body as Ace pulls back just enough to slide his hand between us and play with my clit.

"Oh hell." Between the sensations going on in my lower body, Ace decides to add to them by taking my nipple into his mouth, biting down hard—though not hard enough to hurt me.

My orgasm slams into me like nothing I've felt before.

"That's it, baby, give it to me. Strangle that cock; make it your bitch. Fuck! That feels so. Damned. Good." I feel Ace hammering into me, before I'm flipped over. Ace helps my bone-less body onto my hands and knees, before he slams back into me.

"So deep," I cry out, because it true. No one has ever been this deep before. It helps that Ace is long and hits the sweet spot inside of me. His fingers grip my hips, and I'm sure I will have bruises for days from this. But they're bruises I welcome.

The sound of our skin slapping together fills the room, our love-making fast and furious—ha, love-making… Ace McGowan doesn't make love; he fucks his women. I push down the thought of Ace with other women.

"Come for me again, babe. You can do it." He thrusts forward, harder than he has before, making me move up the bed. His grip bites into my flesh, and it powers my arousal.

"I can't," I whimper. I have never come more than once during sex. But thinking about it, the other men I've been with have been mediocre compared to Ace.

"You can, and you will. I'm going to blow, baby." His thrusts become unsteady as he chases his climax, using my body to do so. His hand leaves my hip and slides around to my clit. One hard pinch and my orgasm flies high.

"That's it, Ana. Climb it—climb it high, baby."

"Ace," I cry out. One, two, three thrusts and Ace climaxes, filling me with his cum. Our heavy breathing surrounds us, the air smelling like sweat and sex. I can feel his heart beating against my back, his trembling body showing evidence of how intense his climax was.

I take a deep breath, my mind swirling with emotions. This past year has been such a journey for me; from dealing with Gary to finally leaving and coming here. Then meeting Nancy, Ace, and the boys of the Unforgiven Riders. Ace forces me to feel things I'm not ready to feel yet.

Should I be moving on so quickly after getting out of a very abusive relationship? Is getting involved with a biker a good idea?

I take a deep breath and turn my head to the side, inhaling deeply, taking Ace's scent into my body, letting it wash over me. Here with Ace I feel safe and loved—even though the words have not been spoken yet. They will soon; I can feel it.

Ace slides off me and settles on the bed, making sure we're touching at all times. The sweaty feel would normally make me gag but being here with him... weirdly it doesn't affect me. He moves me so my head is laying on his chest. He cups the back of my knee, bringing it over his thigh.

"Last, always fucking last," he mutters in a sleepy voice.

"What, honey?" I whisper back.

"I am the last bloke to ever put his cock in this pussy," he says, sliding his hand over my bum, and into my core.

"Oh," I moan.

"Mine, baby. All fucking mine. For now, and *always*." This time his words don't scare the ever-loving crap out of me. Ace has shown me time and time again, with not only me but with Zarah and Nancy, that he will love and protect me.

I let out a contented sigh and relay to him,

"Always, honey. Always last."

His arms tighten around me, caging me against his body. The feeling of contentment and happiness fills me as I drift off to sleep, knowing tomorrow brings a whole new day.

The sun sneaks through the black curtains of Ace's room. I turn my head to see him sleeping on his front, with one arm slung over my belly, holding me in place. We're touching from shoulder to feet. I smile to myself, noticing how relaxed and much younger he looks in a slumber. Ace has always taken the weight of the world on his shoulders, but as the Sergeant-at Arms of the club, that is kinda his job: to not only protect the club, but the families of the club.

I slip out of bed, careful not to wake him. I know he hasn't been sleeping much since Nancy broke the news about her pending death. I look around the room for my dress. I really don't want to wear it downstairs, but I don't think Ace would appreciate me walking downstairs naked. I chuckle at what his reaction would be. He would blow a bloody gasket.

I go to the bathroom and empty my very full bladder, then wash my hands and look at myself in the mirror. I don't look like the scared Ana Dawkins anymore. Ace has impacted my life so much. I'm not sure if he sees it, but I most certainly do. My cheeks have natural colour in them, my eyes seem wide and alive for the first time in years.

I walk over to the dresser and carefully open the top draw, finding underwear and socks. Wow, Ace's drawers are organised. I open the second draw, and it squeaks a little. My head snaps around to make sure my man didn't wake up.

My man.

That feels weird saying. Ace stirs but settles back quickly. I turn back to the dresser and see t-shirts. Ace likes plain t-shirts, no slogans unless it's the club logo.

I pull a club shirt over my head. Lucky for me my boobs are nice and firm, so I can forgo a bra. I close that drawer and open the next. I sigh in relief when I see his jogging bottoms. I pull out a grey pair and slide my legs in, again forgoing my knickers—because no one likes wearing day-old underwear. *Ew.*

I pick up my phone and carefully leave the room, heading downstairs to the kitchen. I turn my phone on and wait for it to boot up. The screen loads and I see it's only just past seven in the morning. I groan in pleasure when I remember I don't have to open the cafe today. I push the kitchen door open and gasp when I see a bare-chested Batch sitting at the table with his daughter resting on his shoulder.

"Morning. I didn't think anyone would be awake," I say as I walk over to put the kettle on.

"It just boiled. This little miss is an early riser when she has colic. She had my mum up most of the night, so I have her so she can get a few more hours of sleep in." Batch's daughter, Grace, is just two months old. Her bitch of a mother left her when she was a few days old. She was more worried about getting her figure back than the actual baby.

"Do you want me to watch her while you get some sleep?"

"Nah, darlin', I'm good—thanks though. I got plenty of sleep last night; the drink knocked me right out." He chuckles.

"If you're sure." I make my cuppa and sit at the table with

him. Grace is a beautiful baby. She has dark, wispy hair like her dad—well, Batch doesn't have wispy hair. His hair reaches just below his ears. It's strange because I've always thought the hairstyle doesn't suit him.

"So how was Ace last night? Did he sleep well, or did you go at it all night long?" He winks at me, making me blush. Grace gurgles, dragging my attention from her unfiltered dad.

"He's fine. I left him sleeping. I know he's been struggling lately." Batch nods while rubbing the baby's back. I smile at the action. "You're a good father, Batch. You'll make a great husband one day." His response surprises me.

"I hope so, babe. I really fucking hope so." My eyes widen at his words.

"Really?"

"Yeah. I'm sick of shagging nameless girls or the club girls. I want to find someone with stability. I have to think of Grace, long term."

"That's good, Batch." I sip my tea, watching him interact with his little girl. She's only a baby but she has all the boys wrapped around her little finger. If one of the club girls come anywhere near her while she's with a brother, she screams the place down.

"Yeah, babe, she needs to come first." He nods down to the baby.

"Call my woman 'babe' once more, fucker, and see what happens," Ace says sleepily as he walks into the kitchen.

"Language, honey. I swear that girl's first word is going to be a swear word." The boys chuckle and Ace leans in and kisses me. Not a quick peck either. He savours the morning kiss.

"Morning, baby. You sleep okay?" he asks as he makes his coffee.

"I did. Did you?"

"Yep, but it was shitty waking up without you. Wake me up next time."

"God, language. Honey, you needed sleep so I left you and

came down here. Do you want breakfast? I can make you boys something."

"You sure, Mouse? It's your day off from the cafe, so I wouldn't expect you to cook for us here."

"Honestly, it's fine, Batch. Full breakfast for you both?" I ask them again.

"Yeah, babe, that'd be great."

I make the boys their breakfast and some for myself. I don't eat like these big oafs. They get the works; bacon, egg, sausage, beans, toast, fried bread, tomatoes and mushrooms. Me, well I have some fruit and yogurt.

We sit and talk for a while, not really anything of special topic —besides Grace's mother has text Batch about seeing her daughter. It's a few hours later when the club start to wake up, and me being the cook of the club, I make a huge amount of breakfast foods for the boys and the old ladies. One or two club girls are still there, but they give us a wide berth.

I rest against Ace, who is leaning against the kitchen counter, and take in the group—no, not group, a family. I see now that I do belong here with them. With Ace McGowan.

Ace

SHIT AROUND THE CLUB HAS BEEN MENTAL. I HAVEN'T SEEN ANA IN three days. I miss her like fucking crazy. The feel of her against me, the taste of her on my tongue, how she manages to leave a lasting impression on my cock for days after it has been inside her... We were happily chilling in her bed, after I had just fucked her in the shower, when Dyson phoned telling me this suit guy had attacked again, this time Eva had been hurt. Not as badly as Sienna, but still hurt.

This fucker is really starting to fuck me off. The boys are all sitting around the large table in the upstairs office, Suede at the head, looking angry as fuck.

"This twat needs to be found and put six feet under. He keeps hurting these girls, but none can catch him. What the hell is up with that?" he bellows out.

"Prez, he's like a fucking ghost. He comes in, makes his play, leaves his mark, and poof... vanishes," EC explains. Suede slams his fist onto the table top, making the table shake. I don't flinch. I'm used to his outbursts. We're all worried about the girls, so much so we've tripled up the boys who guard there at night.

I'm missing *my* fucking girl because I've been here at Silk, watching people, or trying to find this 'suit' via my street connections. I've reached out to a few other MC's, and none of them have been having the same shit as us, so this makes me think it's personal.

"ACE." My names is yelled, but again I don't flinch. I slowly turn my head towards Suede, who's glaring at me. "You listening or not?" I nod. "Well listen up and get your head out of your girl's pussy for five fucking minutes and fill us in on what you've found out."

"One: don't ever refer to my girl's pussy again. Prez, I will knock you the fuck out. Two: the surrounding MC's haven't had fuck all happen to them, so I'm thinking this bloke is targeting Silk because *we* own it. No clue why yet. I'll do some more digging." Suede cocks a bushy brow at me before he speaks.

"Okay, following on your little rant... One: you could fucking try." I smirk at him. "Two: get Click on it too; see what she can drag up." I nod. Click is an old member's daughter. She's only nineteen but she can hack any computer system she gets her hands on. She's protected by the club but doesn't come around the clubhouse much, mainly just for family functions. Her dad is still a patched member but isn't active due to an injury.

I look over to EC and see his face light up at the sound of her name. EC has some hidden feelings for Click, also known as Mae Holden. I cock an eyebrow at him when his gaze catches mine. He smirks at me and rubs his hands over his thighs. EC is one of our younger members, at twenty-two, but the fucking ladies love him, the dirty bastard.

"Dyson, have you checked out the security cameras from the back alley when Eva was attacked?"

"Yeah, can't see fuck all." Rage crosses Dyson's face. Fuck, rage fills us all. These girls are here making a living, not hurting anyone, and some dumb fuck is trying to force them into leaving here and working for him, doing God knows what.

A scream snatches our attention. I slam my chair back and run down the stairs, knowing my brothers are following me. We follow the screams out to the back doorway. Lacey is standing just outside the door. Her hand is over her mouth, her body visibly shaking as she stares down at the floor. I grip her shoulders and shake her making her look at me.

"What happened, Lace?" Her fearful eyes lock on mine, before dropping to the floor again. I follow her gaze and see what has her shaking like a leaf. My stomach rolls, but I force the sensation down.

"Fuck," I mutter, and run my hand over my beard. I close my eyes and try to control my rage.

The boys come barrelling out of the door and all stop in their tracks when they see what I'm seeing.

"Holy shit," Maze mutters, before dropping to Eliza's bloody body. We stand and watch as he checks her pulse. His head drops, and we all know the answer to the next words that will be spoken.

"She's dead," he whispers. We all loved Eliza; she was a good girl. Lacey lets out a full, grunting sob. I turn to look at her, just as she starts to fall to the floor. But Court catches her. He lifts her off her feet.

"Take her up to the office and get a strong drink," Suede tells Court, who nods and steps inside. We all stand around, looking down at Eliza's body. The air is thick, because we know we need to retaliate for this. This fucker needs to be gone. Now.

Maze stands, still looking down.

"We need to call nine-nine-nine, Prez. This is bad. This..." He points down to the body. "We can't hide." Some of the boy's nod in agreement.

"Do it." He turns to Dyson. "Make sure there's nothing dark in there." He points to the club. 'Dark' is our code for anything illegal. Dyson leaves us in the alley to make sure everything is clean inside. Suede pulls out his phone and dials up Officer Daren Horton. He's a friend of the club since we helped him out a few years back with his sister's dickhead husband.

"Dare, we have a situation. I'm letting you know before I dial the numbers. One of the girls at Silk has turned up dead behind the club. We thought we should call it in." With that, he hangs up and dials the officials. Not ten minutes later the sirens fill the air and the red and blue lights flash off the buildings. The police take statements and check over the CCTV footage, but they only see a guy dressed in a black suit. We never see a face.

My anger builds with every passing minute we don't find the guy. I pull out my phone and send a text to Click.

ME: I need you at the clubhouse tomorrow morning.

Click: Hello to you, too, Ace. How are you? I'm okay. Thanks for asking.

ME: Smartarse. There's been another attack at Silks. I need your help, Click.

Click: Who?

ME: Eliza was killed tonight.

Click: I'll be there by eleven. I have a class @9

ME: Nice one.

I lock my phone and put it back in my pocket, before walking around the bar and picking up a bottle of Jack Daniels and taking a mouthful. The liquid burns as it goes down, but then again, the first taste always does. I drink back another, this time savouring the flavour.

I squeeze my eyes shut, forcing the image of the bloody and beaten body of Eliza out of my head. I lift the bottle and tip it back, opening my throat to let the liquid slide down. I don't taste it this time. I just want to forget.

"Slow there, brother," Batch says, taking the stool next to me.

"Nah, don't think I will." Who the fuck does he think he is telling me to slow down?

"So are you planning on getting absolutely smashed and crashing here? With Asia flapping around?" He nods in her direction. Asia is a fucking cunt, plain and simple, but the customers love her. None of the brothers have slept with her because they reckon she's a snake and will swallow them whole.

"Fucking hell." I slide the bottle across the bar towards my brother. He chuckles.

"Yeah, thought so."

"Prick." I climb off the stool and head outside, nodding in the direction of my brothers as I leave. I text Ana to see if she's awake —I need my girl right now—but see it's after three a.m. Bollocks. I climb on my bike and start her up. Maybe a long ride will clear my thoughts.

So much has happened in the last month, and if I'm being honest it's fucking with my head. I'm being pulling in a million fucking directions and something needs to give. We need to find the cocksucker who's hurting the girls so we can go back to a semi-peaceful MC, and I can go to fucking my girl whenever I see fucking fit, and not go for days without seeing her.

My phone vibrates in my pocket, so I pull over to check who it's from. I hope to hell it's from Ana, but my stomach churns when I see it's from Click.

Click: Click the link.

I click on the link and there's a short video clip of a black BMW X5. Three men in suits climb out and step towards Silk. That's where the footage stops, but we get a good look at their faces. My phone dings again. It's another link. I click it and watch again. This time the video shows the same three men in suits walk back to their car, but this time, one of the men has blood covering his shirt and part of his jacket, and both hands.

"Fucking cunt." These are the ones that hurt Eliza. I will fucking find them and put them into the ground. She didn't deserve this. She was hurt because of us; the club. The club will pay for her funeral, since she didn't have any family.

ME: Find them.

I send a text back to Click. I know she won't let me down. She'll find these fuckers. Even though she isn't heavily in the club, she's still very loyal to its members. I send a text to all my brothers telling them to meet me at the clubhouse, so I can tell them what Click found. I tuck my phone away and make my way back to the clubhouse where most of the boys should be waiting for me.

I pull up at the compound and Bull opens the gates for me. I nod at him as I drive in and park my bike next to Dyson's. Knew they would be here. I walk up and push through the door, seeing the room is pretty much empty. Everyone is mourning Eliza. Like I said, she was well liked in the club.

"Everyone's in church, Ace," Ditch says from behind the bar. I walk down the hall to the one room only patched members are allowed to enter. The boys are sitting around the table when I get there. I take a look at each of them, their faces show pure rage over what happened tonight.

Suede bangs the gavel and speaks to the room. "Okay, Ace, you wanted us here. What have you found out?"

"Click found something. She sent CCTV footage of three fuckers in suits. They drive up a few buildings away from Silk. They walk in the club's direction, then a few minutes later they walk back to the car. One suit is covered in blood, blood we can assume is Eliza's."

"Can we get an ID on these wank-stains?"

I nod. "I have Click working on it. You get to see two of the guys' faces. She's running it now. She's also coming to the club tomorrow at eleven to do more digging." I see the boys nod.

"She can do it. She can do fucking anything." EC sings her praises. 'Pussy whipped' gets muttered, and we all laugh. "Fuckers. You all know how good she is at hacking."

"Hell yeah, she is. Just be careful because she may *hack* up her stomach when she sees that tiny cock of yours, since, you know, she's a little nerdy virgin and all. But then again, maybe she does need a big, fat cock to show her the way," Court pipes in from across the table. EC's face goes red, and he slams his chair back as he stands.

"Fuck you, Court. You don't say shit like that about her. I'll slit your fucking throat, I swear to fucking God."

"I'd love to see you try, pretty boy," Court taunts. EC bolts around the table, but Maze catches him before he gets close.

"Enough!" Suede bellows. "Jesus fucking Christ, how old are you two? Fucking toddlers, I tell you. EC, sit the fuck down. Court, shut your trap and stop pissing him off. We know Click don't like the pretty boys anyway." The room erupts into laughter, easing the heavy tension between the two men.

"Piss off, Prez. I don't like her like that, man," EC grumbles, looking down at the table top.

"If you say so, brother," Suede jests back.

We run over a few more things before church comes to a close. I go to my room, declining a drink with the boys. I'm fucking shattered; I need sleep. My eyes burn like hell, my body aches. I close the door behind me and manage to undress before I collapse onto my bed and sleep takes me under.

I dream of my brown-haired girl walking towards me with a beautiful brown-haired little girl.

Ana

FOUR DAYS. FOUR BLOODY DAYS SINCE I'VE SEEN ACE. MY MAN—OR so I thought. He has barely text or called me, and when he does, it's at stupid times of the night when I'm sleeping like the rest of the UK. I shake my head and look down at the menu while Zarah gets our drinks from the bar.

We're at the pub having a meal tonight after working our arses off at the cafe. There is a building being completely renovated in town and all the builders are coming into the cafe throughout the day, wanting food or cold drinks, since we are having a heatwave. Everyone is suffering with it. The UK doesn't know how to cope with this kind of heat. Whether it's hot or cold, the UK shuts down.

My mustard-coloured dress is sticking to my skin because of the heat. I pull a hair-tie out of my bag and put my hair up in a messy bun to keep it off my neck. The bare skin there feels cooler now, and I sigh in relief.

I fiddle with the necklace around my neck. It was a gift from my mum for my birthday one year. It's a simple, thin silver chain, with a pretty silver feather pendant. Zarah got a similar necklace but with a rose pendant.

I reach into my bag and pull out my phone to see if I've had anything from Ace. I can't hide the disappointment when I see there's still nothing from him. Zarah sets our drinks down on the table with a huff.

"Still nothing?" I shake my head. "Typical man. Bloody hell, it's so damn hot in here."

"Don't moan, because you would be moaning if it was raining as well," I snark back, smiling at her before taking a sip of my ice-cold strawberry and lime Kopparberg. You have to drink it with ice.

"True, but we're British and we moan about everything." She winks at me. "So, what are you looking to get to eat?"

"No clue. I'm too hot to eat, but I know I need to eat something." We both sit quietly, looking over the menu. To be honest I think we're both ready to crash for the night. My eyes flick between the menu and my phone sitting on top of the table. I know what's on the menu, I just can't decide what to actually eat. A yawn breaks out and Zarah laughs.

"Tired?"

"Like you wouldn't believe," I answer her.

"Then you need sleep, baby." I close my eyes as his voice laces my body. I shiver as Ace slides into the booth next to me. His arm wraps around my waist, pulling me to him. I turn my head to look at him and take in his handsome face.

He looks tired but happy. His beard needs a trim and he has slight bags under his eyes. I reach up and cup his cheek. Our gazes lock. Ace smiles a smile at me that tells me he missed me, too, but that doesn't stomp out the anger from the loss of contact from him. I drop my hand and turn to face Zarah, who's now sitting next to EC. I didn't even see him sit with us.

"Hey, EC."

"Mouse." That poxy nickname the brothers have given me... I shake my head and smile at him. Ace growls next to me, making EC's smile get wider. He really is a handsome bloke.

"Why the fuck does he get a smile and I don't? I'm your man, not him."

"My man? So why hasn't my man contacted me in three days?"

"Club business," is all he says.

"Well that explains a lot," I say sarcastically. I cross my arms across my chest, and I notice EC's eyes track the movement.

"Hey, fucker. Eyes off, yeah." Ace puts his fingers under my chin and turns my face to meet his gaze. "Baby, we had shit to deal with that I can't fully talk to you about. That is how the club works; you know that." I can hear the tiredness and anguish in his voice. What the hell has happened in the club? See, this is one of the things I dislike about the club. I like to know things, and the club rules say old ladies are to be told shit unless they're in dire need to know the information.

Our gazes are still on each other when I let him know what I'm feeling.

"I hate this, Ace. I hate not knowing what's going on. I like to fix things; you know that. So hearing how bad things are getting in the club and seeing how tired you are, and you can't tell me piss all... it's kinda pissing me off. Call be a brat if you want, but I just want to help." He shakes his head at me and runs his hand over his beard.

"I can't, babe."

"But I want to help, honey. I—" He cuts me off with a vicious growl.

"You can't do fuck all, Ana, so just fucking leave it."

"Ace, I—"

"FUCK! Don't you ever listen? Are you a fucking magician? Can you bring someone back from the dead, huh?" His eyes are blazing with fury, and this time he actually scares me. I shrink back from him. I hear Zarah call my name, but the blackness is closing in. EC yells Ace's name, but I can't focus on them. All I see is black cloud and Ace's angry eyes.

"Ana, baby. Listen to my voice. Come back to me, babe. I'm sorry. Ana."

"Ace, give her room." I can hear their voices, but I can't see them because my eyes won't open. My breathing is laboured, and it feels like an elephant is sitting on my chest. I feel arms wrap around me and that familiar smell hits my senses, and the black fog starts to fade. Lips meet my cheek, then my jaw and then my neck.

"I'm sorry, baby. Open your eyes for me. I'm here, babe. I would never hurt you." I feel myself nodding, but I can't speak as I'm trying to regulate my breathing. I breath deep through my nose and slowly let it out. I do that a few times before I try to open my eyes. Thank God we're in a dimly lit pub. I blink a few times until Ace comes into view, his worried face leaning over me. When did I lay down?

I look around me and see that I am, in fact, on the floor next to our booth, and people are watching us.

"Ignore them, Mouse. Alright, fuckers, show is over," EC barks at the room, and people go back to what they were doing. I see a few women looking over at us. I can only imagine they're eyeing up Ace and EC.

"I need to get up," I breath out. Ace lifts me off my feet and plants me in his lap when he sits in the booth. He brushes the hair off my face and offers me a sad smile.

"I'm so fucking sorry, Ana. I let everything get to me, and I took it out on you when you kept saying you wanted to help. I know you want to help, but, baby, I don't want you to see this side of the club."

"Is it that bad?" Zarah asks from across the table. I look over at my sister, who's looking concerned for me. I smile at her, hopefully portraying that I'm okay.

"Yeah, Z. We lost a club girl a few nights ago. That's all we can say on it," EC explains. I gasp at his words. Oh no, a girl died. Ace's arms tighten around me and any fear from his earlier outburst fades to nothing. I know deep down that he would never hurt me, but there had been so much anger in his eyes...

"We're handling it, okay. The club is paying for the funeral because she had no family."

I lean away from his body slightly. "I want to help." I try to make my voice as steady as possible. I need him to know I'm okay and that I'm not scared of him. He starts to shake his head, but I cup his cheek, making him look at me.

"Yes. I can arrange the food for the wake and help arrange her funeral—flowers and what-not. Please, honey." I plead him with my eyes. His eyes soften, and he leans in and lays a kiss on my lips.

"Bollocks. I can't say no when you call me 'honey' in that tone of voice."

EC coughs, "pussy-whipped", and I turn and shoot him a death glare that wipes the smile off his face. I find it funny that I can silence these boys with the 'mum' glare, even though I'm not a mum yet. Yet. The thought bounces around my head; me carrying Ace's babies. Oh good Lord, they would be bloody beautiful if they looked like their father. Would Ace be a good dad? Oh hell, who am I kidding, of course he would.

"What's got you thinking so hard there, babe."

"Babies," I blurt out. I slap my hand over my mouth and look at Ace with wide eyes.

"And that is our cue to leave, Z. Come on, I'll give you a ride home," EC says, sliding out of the booth and helping my sister out.

"Just a ride home, EC," I warn. He smirks at me, and I go to bitch him out.

"Really, Smallie? I'm a grown woman, ya know. Besides, I don't think this pretty boy here could handle me." Zarah takes a hold of his chin and shakes it a little, in a playful way. But EC being EC can't let her one-up him.

He grabs his crotch and replies,

"Oh, sweetheart, I have plenty for you to handle." He winks at her and Ace groans from my side, resting his forehead on my bare shoulder.

"You really think so, huh?" Zarah steps towards him and his eyes widen. I'm not sure whether that's from being turned on or out of fear. I chuckle until I feel Ace's hands on my jaw, turning me to face him. I don't hear EC or Zarah, or anything in the room. My sole focus is on my man. I lick my lips and watch as Ace's gaze drops to watch the small action.

He leans in and kisses me. His beard scratches and tickles my lips and chin. We get lost in the contact, which happens every time he touches me. He can make everything fade away. Seconds, minutes, pass as the kiss deepens. Until we're brought back to the room, filled with people, by a loud cheer.

"Fuck, babe."

"Yeah," is all I can say, breathless.

I climb off his lap and sit next to him, no space between our bodies.

"Right, now you guys have come up for air, I can tell you we're leaving and pretty boy here will keep his pecker in his jeans and make sure I get home safe," Zarah tells us. I smile at her and she mirrors it. "You deserve this. Make it count."

I nod. "I will. EC, you watch out for my big sister or it'll be your balls on the clubhouse door warning the brothers not to mess with the Dawkins sisters."

"You got it, Mouse. I like my balls firmly attached to my body. Let's move, little sister." He winks at me, and I giggle at him calling Zarah 'little sister', considering she's a few years older than him.

Zarah shakes her head at him but does it with a smile on her face. "Come on, pretty boy, let's get me home so I can have some fun with a very large dildo that knows how to make me come and when to shut himself off." She winks at me, making me and Ace burst into a fit of laughter. The look on EC's face is so comical. His eyes are wide like saucers, and his mouth open and closes like a fish out of water. Zarah steps up to him and taps his cheek, then walks towards the door.

"You need to go after her, brother."

"Did she just... I mean, did she... Fucking hell." Without another word, he turns and follows my sister out of the pub. I wipe the tears leaking from my eyes from laughing. My sister always knows how to put men in their place. She has no filter; she never has. My parents used to encourage us to say what we mean and mean what we say.

"That boy's mouth is going to get him in trouble someday," Ace says.

"In more ways than one." I take a sip from my drink and Ace does the same. We sit in a comfortable silence for a few minutes. Ace slides his arm around my waist, keeping me flush to his hard body. He smells like oil and leather because of his cut and his days of working in the garage.

"How's the cafe doing?"

"Same as always. Busy during the three meal times. It'll get busier when the kids finish for school this summer, but we'll handle it. I may need to hire someone else to help out," I explain to him. He hasn't been in the cafe since Nancy passed away. Not by choice, but because things with the club have kept him busy.

"I know someone that can help out. She can start whenever you need her to. She's a good girl. I know she'll be happy to help." I know I shouldn't feel like it, but jealousy creeps in. Is she one of his girls from before me? Does she want Ace to be hers? Is that why she'll help when he asks?

Ace must see the questions running around my head by the look on my face. He grips my chin and tilts my head to look me in the eyes.

"Baby, no. Stop thinking that fucked up shit. She's the daughter of a non-active member. She's nineteen and is a pretty cool kid. Her name is Mae, but we call her 'Click' because she's a fucking whizz at all that computer shit." I let out a sigh, and the feeling of guilt settles in my belly for doubting him.

"I'm sorry for thinking any different. I'm trying here, honey." He leans in and kisses me gently. "I know, babe. Click will be a good addition. Plus, it's a way to keep an extra eye on her, and she gets cash in her pocket. Not that she needs it."

"Okay, send her round to us. Is she pretty?" His smile takes over his face, his white teeth showing through the brown hair of his beard.

"She's a beauty. The boys will go wild for her. One in particular will be visiting more than he usually does." I frown at him and he chuckles. Who does he mean? Like he can hear the question in my head, he speaks up. "EC, baby."

I gasp. "Really?" He nods.

"Yep. He's had a thing for her since he joined the club, but since he was a prospect, he couldn't touch her. Then he got his patch, but she had a boyfriend. They've had this cat and mouse thing going on for a while now."

"I know something about that." I smile at him.

"EC thinks he will hurt her, so he kept his distance, but Click didn't care. She turned up the heat to get him, but he fucked up. She came to the club just after her eighteenth birthday, only to find EC getting his dick sucked by a club girl." I gasp. The poor girl. "Click never came around after that, and she gave up chasing him. That hit him hard, and then he started fucking anything with a pussy."

"Oh, it must be hard for them both. Him for wanting her but knowing he messed up, and for her to remember how much he hurt her yet know she has to see him from time to time." I rest my hand over my heart, willing my old romantic heart to find a way to fix them.

"Don't do it, sweetheart,"

"Do what?" I feign innocence.

"You know what." I smirk at him and push him to move out of

the booth. He frowns at me, but I give him a seductive smile
—hopefully.

"Let's go. Take me home, Ace. I want to feel you inside me."

That's all it takes for him to leap from the booth, pulling me
behind him. We make it home on his bike in no time.

I take it when you promise Ace McGowan a good time, the
man wastes no time in getting it. Good to know.

Ace

I KICK THE DOOR SHUT BEHIND ME AND I CARRY ANA TO MY bedroom. I brought her to my home and not the clubhouse. I don't want those fuckers saying shit about Ana screaming my name, because she will be screaming my name.

My house is thirty minutes from the city centre and fifteen minutes from the clubhouse. It comes in handy to be close to everything, for moments like this.

I lower her so her feet meet the floor, but I keep her body firmly against me. Our gazes are blazing with lust and want. I slam my mouth against hers and take the kiss I've wanted to take since she walked into the cafe that winter morning.

She breaks the kiss and pushes me so I fall onto the bed. I go up on my elbows and look up at her. Her eyes are filled with desire and want for me—for my cock.

"What do you want, baby?"

"You know what I want," she answers.

"Then come and get it, babe. He's right here. Waiting for you." I nod down towards my rock-hard dick in my dark jeans. Ana slowly lowers herself to her knees, and I thank fucking God that I laid carpet in this room. How the hell I let her control the situation when her tiny fingers open my jeans and take out my dick, I have no fucking idea. I deserve a medal for this shit.

I moan when her hand wraps around my cock, slowly moving up and down. My head falls back between my shoulders. "Mouth, baby. I need your fucking mouth on me."

Thank fuck she listens to me. Clearly the want is loud in my voice. My head snaps up to see her perfect pink lips wrap around the head of my cock, but she doesn't stay there. She grips my shaft and runs her tongue around my balls, moving them around before sucking one into her warm mouth.

"Oh fuck. Yeah, baby, suck it. Yeah, now the other one." I force my arms to stay up, so I can watch as she sucks and licks my balls. They tingle to high heaven. "Fuck," I growl as she sucks one into her mouth. Hard.

"Put my dick in your mouth, babe. I wanna see your lips wrapped around my cock." I watch as she licks the head of my dick first, tasting the precum that's formed there. Her gaze connects with mine as she opens her mouth and sucks the head of my shaft. My balls tighten, and I shiver. A sly smile covers her face when she sees how I react to her.

"Suck it hard and all the way back, babe," I demand. Eyes still on me, she lowers her mouth on me, taking every inch until I hit the back of her throat. Ana gags a little but swallows through it, making me grit my teeth. "Fuck, that feels good."

I know if I don't stop this now, I'm going to come down her throat and not in her pussy. I watch as her head bobs up and down my dick, her saliva dripping down onto my balls. God, this is a fucking sight to behold. I lean forward and slide the yellow straps of her dress off her shoulder, one by one. She isn't wearing a bra. Her tits sit firmly in the cups of the dress. I move forward more, effectively forcing my dick out of her mouth.

"You okay? Am I not doing it right?" She looks up at me with concerned eyes.

I cup her chin and lay a kiss on her mouth, tasting myself on her lips.

"You were perfect. Too fucking perfect. I was going to come down your throat if you didn't stop, baby, and I want to come in that pretty pussy of yours. Stand up," I command, and she listens. Ana likes to be told what to do. Not in an aggressive way, but in a very sexual way.

I watch as she climbs to her feet, using my thighs as leverage. I look up at her and take in her beauty. Some of her brown hair has come loose from her hair-tie thing, and her lips are puffy from being wrapped around my dick. Her eyes are glazed over with desire for me to fuck her into next week. To take her high with every orgasm I'm going to give her.

I slide my hands up the back of her thighs, over the curve of her arse, feeling the cotton knickers with a little lace trim on them. I slip my fingers under the material, feeling the smooth skin of her arse, and squeeze,

"Ace." She moans my name, making my cock jerk between us. I move my hands, so I can pull her knickers down her long legs. I look up when she gasps, and smirk at her.

"Lose the dress, babe." I lean back on my elbows again and enjoy the view of my girls stripping for me. Ana is so fucking reserved. It's fucking crazy that we fit together. My gaze moves from hers as the dress slowly glides down her body. It slides over her tits like melting chocolate. I watch as it lands on the floor, settling at her bare feet.

"Fuck me, you are beautiful." My voice comes out hoarse and full of emotion, seeing my woman naked before me. When we first had sex in my room at the clubhouse, I didn't take the time to fully appreciate her body.

"Hair down." She lifts her arms up and unties her hair. The colour of her hair is a stark contrast to her pale skin. I watch as her tits move with the raising of her arms. I run my eyes over her body and find that she's fucking perfect in my eyes. Including the small scar I missed before, sitting on her hip. I reach out and touch it. She recoils from my touch and my gaze snaps to hers.

"Who put it there? What happened?" I demand, gripping her hips with both hands, holding her in place.

"Leave it, Ace. It's nothing." Her hands settle on my shoulders, pushing me back, so I'm laying down. I watch as her eyes plead with me to let it go, so I do. For now. "You will tell me some day." She nods and pulls my jeans down over my thighs.

"Up." She indicates that she wants me to lift my hips. I do as she asks.

My jeans meet the carpet, and I watch as my woman climbs me like a fucking tree. She straddles me, her pussy resting on my dick. I'm pretty fucking sure she loves to torture me with that hot, slick centre.

"T-shirt, honey." Her voice drops into that seductive tone she uses when she wants something. She pushes the bottom of my shirt up my stomach, keeping her palms on my skin. I reach behind my neck and tug the material over my head, before flinging it across the room, not giving a fuck where it lands.

My eyes zone in on the apex of her thighs as she reaches for my shaft and lowers herself down on me. My back arches and my head pushes into the bedding as the feel of total fucking bliss fills my body. The feel of her soft, warm pussy taking me, makes me wanna preach to the fucking God almighty. But that fucker isn't making me feel this good. No, it's my woman riding the fuck out of my dick.

I feel her lips on my neck as I arch back from the sensations racing through my body.

"Hell yeah, baby. Ride that cock—take your pleasure. God."

"Yes, honey. God, you feel so good inside me." I let her have her few minutes of control before I flip us over. Then she's on her knees and I'm slamming into her from behind. I reach forward, cupping her jaw, forcing her to turn her head to face me. Our gazes lock, and I slowly lower my hand, gripping her throat and leaning in so I can kiss her puffy lips.

I catch her moan with my mouth, and I pound into her, my hips meeting her lush arse. She snags my wrist with her tiny hand.

I slow my movements, dipping my hips, grinding into her rather than pounding. "You okay?" I whisper in her ear. She gives me a jerky nod, letting me know I can pick the pace up again.

"God, baby, you feel so good." Her knees give out until she's lying flat on her stomach. I adjust her left leg, bending it at the knee. I climb onto the bed, practically mounting her. I place one knee on the bed and one foot by her hip and start to slam into her.

"Har-harder, Ace."

"Like this?" I slide my dick almost all the way out and slam back in so fucking hard we move up the bed. The bedding is crumpled up in her fists, her knuckles turning white. She's holding on so tight.

"Yes!" Her screams fill the room. "Again." I repeat the movement, and I can feel my balls tighten and my spine start to tingle. I pull out because I want to see her face as she comes.

I flip her over and hold her ankles in the air, before sliding home again. Sliding in deep makes us moan in pure lust.

"Fuck, I'm gonna come," she pants out. I use my left hand to pinch her clit, sending her over the edge. She screams my name as her orgasm sweeps through her body. Her chest gets a flushed look as I keep up the steady pace, dragging every ounce her of climax from her.

Her body sags when the twitching of her pussy calms, and I don't waste any time chasing my own orgasm. I slam in once, twice.

"Baby, where do you want me to come?"

Her eyes snap to mine, and her red cheeks rise with her sexy smile.

"Mouth."

"Fuck yeah, get ready, baby. Yes." I can feel my climax reaching its peak. I pull out and Ana quickly lays on her stomach, takes my dick in her mouth, and sucks hard.

"FUCK," I growl as my orgasm shoots out the head of my dick and straight into her willing mouth. Spurt after spurt, my cum fills her mouth, and she swallows like a fucking pro.

I'm breathing heavy when I collapse onto the bed beside her. Ana crawls up the bed and lays next to me.

"That was—"

"Fucking amazing," I answer for her. She tilts her head and kisses my chest.

"Why did we wait so long, Ace?" I get what she's asking, but is she ready to hear my answer? Because in reality, it was her fault we waited. Fuck it, she has to know.

"You tell me, babe. I was after you, but you kept me away. Only you can answer your own question."

"I had a lot going on, Ace, and to be honest, I had seen you with multiple women. You can't blame me for not letting you make a move on me."

"What did you have going on?"

"Just daily things." She buries her body deep into mine, like she can't get close enough.

"Why don't you talk about your past to me? I want to know everything, Ana."

She doesn't speak right away. She lets the question hang in the air between us. "I know you do, honey. Please give me some time. I'll tell you everything, okay? I promise."

"Soon, very fucking soon, Ana." She nods and yawns, making me chuckle. "Did I wear my baby out?" She nods again. I move us up the bed so we're laying on the pillows. I manoeuvre our bodies and pull the blankets over us.

"Sleep, baby."

"M'kay," she answers in a groggy voice, already almost out. Having her in my arms feels right. This is only place she belongs:

here with me. No other man will get to touch her. Now that she's my old lady, the club will always protect her like they would me.

I need to put a call in to Sketch and make an appointment for us to get our property tattoos done. Zarah has warned me Ana is deathly afraid of needles, so we'll have to see if Sketch can advise on that. But she is getting it done. I need people to know who the fuck she belongs to.

I wrap my arms around my girl and fall into a deep sleep, feeling like the king of the world.

Ana

I wipe the table down and carry the dirty dishes into the kitchen. I place them in the dishwasher and start it up. We are run off our feet again today. The builders have been pouring in at a steady pace during the day. A few have hit on me and Zarah, but when the prospect growls in their direction they quit the flirting, making us both laugh. Ditch has been sat in the corner since we opened this morning, but from the look on his face, he's none too happy about it. But hey, he wanted to prospect for the club.

The bell above the door dings and I lift my head to see who has walked in. A squeal comes from behind me before I even register who is by the door. Zarah comes running from behind the counter and makes a beeline for Theo.

Holy cow, it's Theo.

I run and join them in a big hug. Theo is our first cousin on our mother's side. He's the same age as Zarah. My family kept their distance because of Gary.

Gary.

I pull back and frown at Theo, then look behind him to see if Gary is outside the cafe window. I know I'm being silly, but the thought of him finding me makes me feel sick to my stomach.

"How did you know where we were, Theo?" My voice is calm, but inside I'm shaking.

"This one let slip about the funeral you went to." He pulls Zarah tighter to him. My gaze snaps to hers, and she cringes when she sees my face.

"Why? How? We have been so bloody careful, Zarah. Bloody hell." I rest my hand over my forehead and close my eyes, taking deep breaths. I open my eyes to see how upset my sister is. "Were you followed, Theo?"

I pull Zarah in for a hug to reassure her we're fine. She wraps her arms around me, squeezing the life out of me.

"Only I know. I've taken two weeks off work for a holiday. I spent time travelling up the coast, surfing and what-not." Oh, did I forget to mention Theo was a surfer? Yeah, he has the tan, the abs, and the shaggy blonde hair to go with it.

"So you ended up here?" I ask cautiously.

"Yeah, baby-A. If anyone was following me, they would have got bored watching me surf and pull some hot chicks on the way. Well, they wouldn't have got bored of the shows we put on, but hey..." He winks at me and I laugh. I hear the rumble of the bikes before I see them. I can now tell there are at least four bikes by the different sounds of the exhausts.

I look over to where Ditch is sitting, and he's scowling at Theo. Oh hell.

"You didn't?" He just shrugs at me. Yes, he did. I stand there and watch as Ace, Batch, Dyson and Court dismount their bikes and make their way in. Ace leading the pack.

I place my hands on my hips and wait for him to close the small distance, as we are standing right in front of the door. Ace's eyes flicker between me and Theo, who still has his arm around my shoulder.

"You wanna tell me why the fuck you have your arm around my woman?" Ace fumes. No 'Hello Ana'. No 'How are you, babe'. Nada.

Poxy alpha biker men.

"Well hello to you, too, Ace," I mutter. His gaze snaps to mine before returning to Theo. The thing about the Dawkins men... they don't back down.

"And who are you?" Theo asks Ace, puffing out his chest. He takes a step forward, gently pushing me behind him. He thinks I need protection from these boys; from Ace.

"Theo, he's—"

Ace's bellow cuts me off. "Who am I? Who the fuck am I? I'll tell you who the fuck I am. I'm her old man, and she's my old lady, so I suggest you take your grubby fucking paws off my property. NOW!"

Theo bursts out laughing and steps forward with his hand raised to shake Ace's. I smile at the action, but the brothers of the Unforgiven Riders look at Theo like he's lost his bloody mind.

"Well why didn't you lead with that, you tit. I'm Theo, Zarah and *Ana's cousin.*" His hand is still mid-air, waiting for Ace to shake it, but he just stares at the hand and then back up to Theo's face.

"Ace," I prompt. He looks at me, and I frown at him before dropping my eyes to Theo's hand. Luckily, Ace shakes it.

"Nice to meet you. I see that my cousins have all the protection they will ever need."

"Damn right they do," Dyson chimes in from behind Ace. "They belong to the Unforgiven Riders and the club will protect them." Theo chuckles, making me look at him.

"Boys, there is something you need to learn about the Dawkins ladies. They don't like to be owned by *anyone.*"

"That's where you're wrong, mate. Ana belongs to Ace," Dyson explains. Theo looks between Ace and me, waiting for an explanation. I step closer to Ace and slide my arm around his waist. Theo's eyes widen, but he doesn't say anything right away.

"They're right, cousin. I'm with Ace. I'm his old lady, and in the eyes of the club, it's an honour to have such a title. The 'owned' part is in the club words only. Ace would never tell me what to do, unless it was to keep me safe." Ace places his arm around my shoulders, keeping me tucked against him. I can see Theo thinking things over in his head, his eyes bouncing between Ace and me and over to the brothers.

"Honestly, Theo, they would never hurt us. They aren't that kind of MC. They're big softies really," Zarah tells Theo, winking at the boys.

"Softies? Really, Z? I can show you hard if you believe I'm soft for you." Batch say, then winks.

"Batch." Ace says his name in warning.

"It's all good, brother. She knows I'm kidding, don't you, Z?" He bounces his eyebrows at my sister.

"Oh good lord." I turn into Ace's chest, giggling.

"If you say so, Batchy boy." Zarah loves winding the boys up. "Come and have a coffee, Theo. Maybe if you're lucky I'll throw in some of my cake as well."

"I want a slice of your cake, baby."

"Are they always like this?" Theo asks as we watch Batch trail after Zarah towards the cafe counter. We know nothing will happen because they respect Zarah and me. The banter between them is so funny.

"Pretty much, yeah. You hungry? Grab a seat with the boys and I'll bring you something." I look up at Ace and kiss his neck, just where his beard stops. "You want something too, honey?"

Ace gives me the smile that will melt the knickers off any woman within a ten-mile radius. "Yeah, babe. You know what I like. Come sit, man," he says to Theo. The boys go and sit in the corner where Ditch is looking at me.

"No cake for you, sunshine." I point at him. He juts out his bottom lip, pouting.

"Come on, Mouse. I was only looking out for you and Z. I didn't know who the bloke was."

"You have a mouth, use it from time to time and ask a question."

"My mouth has plenty of uses, Mouse, but asking questions isn't one of them." I palm my forehead and smile at him.

"I walked right into that one, didn't I?"

"Yeah, baby, you did." Ace answers for him and all the guys laugh. I leave them laughing behind me and go to help Zarah. I sort the boys their favourites and take it over to the table. Ace helps me hand the food out, ever the biker gentleman. I kiss the top of his head when he sits back down.

"Do you boys need anything else?"

A round of 'no's' and 'I'm good' have me going to stepping away to finish helping out in the cafe. We're only open for another hour or so.

I clean up as the time moves forward. I watch the boys chat and banter back and forth. Ace lifts his eyes to me, and he gives me a smile that makes my knees weak and my knickers wet. He throws me a wink and I bite my bottom lip, knowing it drives him crazy.

I see him shift in his seat, and I quickly take the tray in my hand into the kitchen. I'm bent over the dishwasher when I feel two arms wrap around me. I squeal as he pushes me forward against the counter.

"You teasing me, baby?"

"No," I answer, my voice just a little high, not hiding the lie.

"I think you were. Now you know how I feel about you teasing me." I shake my head and he chuckles. "Teasing only gets you a good, hard fuck, babe. Thanks to that little lip biting action out there, you can feel what you've done to me. So now you have to take care of him, before he busts through my jeans and shows the boys up with how much bigger than them he is." I snigger.

I can feel how hard he is by the way he's pressing his erection into my backside. I push back, just to drive him that little more crazy, but Ace doesn't like being teased—as he said.

His hands leave my waist and slide up the outside of my thigh, taking my pink and white embroidered dress with them. One hand latches onto my hip, while the other slides effortlessly into the front of my pink satin knickers.

"Are you wet for me, sweetheart?" His fingers slide lower, towards my entrance.

"Maybe," I tease. I'm deliciously punished with a pinch to the clit. I moan his name.

"No maybe. You're soaked and ready for me." His fingers move at an agonisingly slow pace over my clit. One hand leaves my body, and I hear a zipper being pulled down. My head snaps towards the open door that leads out to the cafe. Anyone can just walk in. People will hear him take me.

"Ace, no—"

"Yes." I feel him line his shaft up against me before sliding inside me. He takes his time, like he has other places to be in the world. His thrusts are controlled and deep. I lean forward onto the worktop, keeping my palms flat on the surface, his fingers still dragging sensations out of my clit, making my body buzz with arousal.

"Ace." I breath out his name.

"I can feel you starting to tighten, babe. You need to come fast before someone walks in on us." His thrusts become deeper and faster, his fingers matching the new pace. I look to my left, eyeing the door, praying no one walks in or hears me. His fingers press down hard, and I slam my hand over my mouth to stop the scream from leaving me. This isn't me. I don't ever do things like this. What is this sexy man doing to me?

"Come, Ana. Now." As if his words have control over my body, my orgasm slams into me. My knees go weak, but Ace holds me up as the pulsing beats through my body. One bolt after another.

"Good girl. Hold on, this will be hard and fast." He picks up the pace, slamming into me over and over again, chasing his orgasm. My body is being jolted against the unit as Ace powers through his orgasm with a growl in my neck.

"Fuck, that was good. So fucking good." He kisses my neck and pulls out of me. A whimper leaves my lips. I rest my head on the worktop, trying to catch my breath. I jump when I feel a cool, damp cloth between my legs. Ace is cleaning me up. God, I love this man.

Shit. Ohmygod!

"Thanks," I mutter, unable to meet his eyes. I adjust my knickers, even though Ace pulled them back into place. My dress is a little wrinkled, so I run my hands down, smoothing the material. Eyeing the sink, I walk over to wash my hands, even though I didn't really touch anything.

It's strange falling in love with someone again. Gary hurt me so bad, both mentally and physically. I never thought I would find love again, and then this bearded, tattooed biker came charging into my life, making me feel things I was too scared to feel.

"Hey, you okay"? he asks as he wrap his arms around me again.

"Yeah," I whisper.

"You don't look or sound okay. Did I hurt you?" I turn around to face him. I look up at him and take in the tender look on his face. Who would have thought this rough and ready-looking biker could be gentle?

"I'm good. I promise." I need to tell him how I feel. "Come over to mine tomorrow. I'll do a barbecue for everyone, since Theo is here." He smiles at me, but he's also assessing me before he answers.

"Yeah, babe. Sounds like a plan."

"Good. Now get out of here, so we can clean up and go home. I'm so tired."

"Okay, babe. Get some rest. I'll see you a bit later when I'm done with club business."

"You don't have to come over, Ace."

"I will be there later." He kisses me and walks out of the kitchen, leaving me to my thoughts that I do, in fact, love Ace McGowan.

Ace

Sitting on the back decking of my place, watching some of my brothers talk with Ana, Zarah, and their cousin, Theo, my heart swells. Ana wanted us to have this barbecue at her place, but I know how rowdy the boys can get after a few beers. So I offered to have it here instead. Suede is handling the grill, but Ana made everything else, since this was her idea.

My eyes are glued to my girl when a bottle of beer is placed in my line of sight. I look up to see Lola smiling down at me. Without hesitation, she sits next to me.

"Have you told her yet?" I shake my head. I know I need to tell her how I feel, and I'm pretty fucking sure she feels the same way. Ana isn't a fling kinda girl. She wants it all, and I'm going to give it to her.

"You talked to Sketch? She needs to be booked in."

"Yeah, he's coming today. He should be here soon. She's shit scared of needles."

"Oh, bless her heart. I'm sure Sketch will help calm her nerves. He's good like that. She also needs her property cut, hun." I nod because she's right. Sketch is fucking awesome at talking to people and helping to get them ready for a new tattoo, plus I need to order her cut. The one that will say:

'Property of Ace".

As if on cue, Sketch comes strutting through the side gate. I smile and climb to my feet, then make my way over to him. I've known Sketch since we were in primary school.

"Hey, you sexy bastard." Oh, I forget to mention Sketch is as gay as they come, but you would never tell by the way he looks or carries himself. His arms are covered in tattoos, from his knuckles to his chest. His back is completely covered.

"Hey, fucker." We hug it out man to man style. That's the one thing I love about my club: we don't give a fuck about anyone's sexual orientation. Where you get your dick wet it completely up to you—or who you rub your pussy against.

Fuck, my cock thickens in my jeans as I think of Ana and another woman rubbing their pussies together. I wonder if she would do that for me.

"So where is this woman you had to bribe into being your old lady, then? I hear she's a beaut." I smirk at him and point over to Ana. As if she senses me, she looks my way and smiles at me, giving a little wave. I crook my finger at her, beckoning her to me.

"Holy fucking hells bells. That's her?" Sketch asks from beside me. I nod at him.

Ana steps up to us, sliding her arm around my waist, and I wrap my arm around her shoulders, pulling her to me. I lean down to kiss her lips.

"Baby, this is my lifelong friend, Sketch. Sketch, this my Ana, my old lady."

"Fuck me. What the hell are you doing with this ugly fucker? You are way too hot to be with him," Sketch jokes. Ana blushes to high heaven and buries her head in my chest to hide her embarrassment.

"Says the guy who wanted to suck my dick at the tender age for fourteen," I jest back, smirking at him. Ana's head snaps up, and she looks between both of us, wondering if she heard me right.

"In my defence, I was a very horny teenage boy then." He winks at Ana.

"Then? Dude, you're always horny."

"True." He turns to look at Ana and lifts his arms out. "It's nice to finally meet you, Ana." He pulls her into a hug before releasing her back to me. "Okay, so now the pleasantries are done, why don't we get down to why I'm actually here," Sketch says, and Ana tenses next to me.

"I told Sketch you're scared of needles, so he's going to walk you through everything." She looks up at me with fear in her eyes. I cup her cheeks with my hand and make her look at me. "Baby, I'll be with you all the way. Sketch is the best. He'll make it as painless as possible. I promise."

"I'm not gonna lie to you, Ana, it will hurt, but it depends where you will be having the tat."

"My wrist," Ana whispers. She clears her throat and speaks again, but in a stronger tone this time. "My wrist, please."

"Okay, that will cause you some pain, but again it will depend on your pain threshold. Do you have the design?" He looks at me, and I nod.

"Yeah, Ana is having something pretty but linked to the club. You know how Suede is with the club ink."

He nods. "Tell me."

"I want the club's skull, but with some roses sitting on the bottom, and Ace's name." Her voice shakes a little. Clearly she's still shit-scared to get this done. But if she wants to be my old lady, she has to wear my patch.

"Wicked. I can do that."

"Round up, lads. We have some shit coming our way," Suede bellows across the garden. My eyes find his and he shakes his head. The look on his face tells me it's bad. Sketch stands stock still, because even he can tell it's something bad.

I turn to Ana, and I can see the fear is back on her face. I cup her cheek and lean in for a kiss. She sighs against me and I deepen the kiss. Fuck knows when I will see her again. These 'suit' fuckers need to be put down. My tongue plays with hers, tasting the cupcake she ate earlier.

"ACE!" Fuck. I pull back and rest my forehead against hers, breathing her in.

"I have to go, baby. I'll come back to you as soon as I can. I'll text later tonight, okay?" She nods.

"Please, be safe."

"Always, baby." I kiss her again. The boys walk past us, each giving Ana a kiss on the cheek once they've kissed Lola. I growl, and each of the soon-to-be-dead brothers winks or smirks at her. Sketch full out laughs at us. Court is the last to make a move, but he goes for her lips and not her cheek. Ana is too stunned to stop it.

I lunge for him and slam my fist into his jaw.

"Mine, you dumb fuck." He smirks at me, rubbing his jaw.

"Just making sure." He winks at Ana, and she scowls at him.

I lean in and hiss her cheek, then her lips. "Always—"

"Last," she finishes for me.

"Yeah, babe." With one last look at her, I follow my brothers out of the garden and to our bikes.

We're all sitting around the table in church, waiting for Prez to fill us in. His hand's running through his long beard, proving to me he's nervous and pissed.

"The suits turned up at Silk. Click managed to do her thing and track down some info on these fuckers, but she's still digging for a location."

"We went over some shit when she popped in the other day. But we still couldn't get an ID on the pricks."

"What did they want?" Maze asks.

"He wants the girls and the business. He says he works in skin and he wants our girls. He knows Silk is doing well. He also said something about getting back what's his. That he needs to cleanse it since we tainted it."

"What the fuck is that supposed to mean?" Court grunts.

"No fucking clue, brother."

"EC, you stick your dick in a married woman again?" Batch jests from across the table.

"Haha, funny fucker. No. And that happened once, man, come on."

"So what are we going to do about this guy?"

"We keep the fucker away from Silk. He's not taking the girls or the club. That is Unforgiven Riders property. Get Click to work her magic, double time. We need to find them and run them out of our territory."

"And run them into the ground," Court grinds out.

"Hell yeah," Maze adds.

"I'll get in touch with Click again and see what she can dig up."

"How are the girls, Batch?"

"Recovering. Sienna is talking about visiting family up north. I'll give her some money if she wants to go." Suede nods in agreement. We always take care of our girls.

"Maze, how are the numbers looking?" Suede asks. Maze is the club's treasurer and makes sure we stay in the black where money is concerned.

"Great, actually. The club, bar and cafe are taking in good money. Everything is looking stable at the moment."

"Batch, how's the business going?"

"Awesome as always. We have a few big contracts coming up." He runs his hands through his hair. I smile to myself, thinking how Ana always says that his hair doesn't suit him.

"Nice. Anything else, lads?" Suede asks around the table. Everyone shakes their head, and he bangs the gavel down, ending church for today.

We all stand and make our way out to the bar for a drink—well, I need a fucking drink. I tap the bar and a prospect brings be a bottle. I down half in one gulp. The cold liquid feels good running down my throat. I feel a hand on my back, and turn my head to see Clover standing there smiling at me. Her eyes are running up and down my body like she's a starving woman.

"Can I help you with something?"

"I haven't seen you in ages. I was wondering if you wanted to catch up? You know, the way we used to."

I lean away from her and give her a serious look. "And why the hell would you think I want to hang out like we used to? I have an old lady now."

"Where is she, Ace?" She looks around the room for Ana.

"She's working. You know, keeping the cafe running."

"Come to my room, babe. She won't know." She runs her fingers down my arm, tracing my tattoos like Ana does. I move my arm and go to tell her where she can go, but my phone dings in my pocket. I pull it out and see a text from Click.

Click: Found them. Map and address are attached.

Me: Got it. Thanks, sweetheart.

"Church," I bellow, making sure every fucking brother hears me. Suede comes storming out of the kitchen.

"What the fuck, boy?"

"Click did her magic," is all I say, and make my way back into church.

Three hours later, we're sitting in the mud and grass, watching a bunch of fuckheads come and go into an old warehouse just outside of town. The guys in suits arrived about an hour ago. Two girls were being dragged in behind them by four scruffy-looking lads.

"We need to make a move," Court whisper-yells at me. I shake my head.

"Not yet. We need more intel, for fucks sake. Calm your tits, will you."

"They hurt our girls, Ace."

"You think I don't fucking know that, man. Fuck." I know all the boys are out for blood—fuck, so am I—but we need to be smart about this.

He punches the ground beneath him out of anger and frustration. Court is the one you don't want to piss off. He has a foul temper when he gets going. One time a sister chapter came to visit and one of the brother's got up in Court's face. He laid the bastard out, It took six of us to pull him off the man, otherwise he would have killed him.

"I know, brother. I know."

"That's it for tonight, boys. We've seen all I think we will see. Let's get some sleep and meet in church at ten tomorrow. We'll make a plan then."

We all agree and make our way over to our bikes. We parked them down the road, so they wouldn't be heard. I pull out my phone to check the time. Fuck, it's gone one a.m. Ana will be sleeping already. Fucking hell.

I follow my brothers to the clubhouse. We all park up and go our separate ways. I ignore the look Clover is giving me and go straight to my room. I need sleep. I think about sending my girl a text but worry it might wake her up, so I don't bother. I'll call her tomorrow.

Sleep comes easy as I am tired as fuck. Running around for the club has tired me the fuck out. I just hope I get to see my girl tomorrow.

Ana

I SPOON THE REST OF THE CHILLI INTO THE STORAGE BOX AND SEAL the lid on top. I place that in the bag with the rest of the food and snacks I've made for the boys. I haven't seen Ace in three days. I've had a total of four texts, and that pisses me off, but I know the club is dealing with some nasty stuff. But still, it takes ten seconds to send me a quick text. Ditch doesn't give away any information when I ask him.

I load up the two bags into my car and drive to the clubhouse. I stop by the gate and Bull opens it for me, giving me a silent nod. I park my car and turn the engine off, before climbing out and getting the bags out of the boot. I smile and wave to some of the boys who are working in the garage.

Pushing the door to the clubhouse open with my hands full seems a struggle, but I manage.

I see Bear behind the bar and give him a smile.

"Hey, Bear, do you know where Ace is?" He won't meet my eyes, and my heart starts to race. "Bear?" I ask again when he doesn't answer me.

"He's busy with club business at the moment, Mouse," he explains, while rubbing the back of his neck. Don't men realise they do that when they're nervous?

"He's in his office, right?"

"Mouse." He says my nickname but doesn't tell me where Ace is. With each passing second, my heart sinks more.

"Tell me." He must take pity on me, and he knows his brother is about to get caught doing God-knows-what. He takes a deep breath and nods. I can only imagine that he doesn't want me to see whatever Ace is up to. My heart is racing a mile a minute. My palms become sweaty and I adjust the bags I'm holding. I stop at the office door and hear a giggle behind the wood. My heart drops into my shoes.

Placing the bags on the floor, I wipe the sweat off my hands, into my dress I wore especially for him. I slowly turn the handle and push the door open. The scene before me has my heart breaking and my eyes filling with tears.

Ace is sat at his desk chair, and Clover's bending over him in just a pair of knickers. Her knee is resting on the chair between Ace's thighs. He's looking up at her, not actually touching her, while talking with a smirk on his face. The smirk he gives me when he wants something from me. But I guess... not anymore.

"I guess I'm not needed anymore," I declare. Ace's body snaps to attention and looks around the skank in front of him. His eyes narrow, and he forces her aside, but I don't wait around to see what he has to say. He just broke us.

I storm out of the clubhouse, leaving the bags of food behind. I hope he fucking chokes on every bite. My palms slam against the door and I burst out into the sunlight. I can hear him screaming my name, but I don't stop. I need to get away from him. I need to fucking leave this place. Leave the cafe. A sob breaks free when I feel myself being pulled to a stop.

"When I call your name, you fucking stop," he yells at me.

"I don't, Ace. Go back to your little whore. I'm going home." I step towards my car, but he roars my name.

"ANA!" I spin around to face him, yelling back at him.

"WHAT?" My breathing is coming in heavy pants. I fear I will pass out if I don't get control of it.

"Careful what you say, woman, and remember who you're talking to," he growls at me. I let out a laugh and lock gazes with him, ignoring the boys from the garage who are now watching the show.

"Oh, I know who you are. You're the man who swore up and down that he would never fucking hurt me. The man who I kept at arm's length for fear of him hurting me. And you did it anyway. I told you. I fucking told you, *and you cheated on me!*" My anger is overtaking my hurt at this moment. I can only imagine how much this will hurt when I get home and make plans to leave. I swipe the tears away angrily. This man—no man—should ever make the woman he is with, cry.

"I didn't fucking cheat on you."

"But you would have if I hadn't interrupted you both in there." I point at the clubhouse. I step back towards my car.

"That is fucking bullshit and you know it. I was pushing her away." I shake my head in disbelief at his explanation. His fists are clenching and unclenching, but that doesn't scare me because I know that no matter how angry Ace is, he would *never* lay a hand on me.

"Do you actually expect me to believe that? I stood there for a few seconds before I spoke up. You were trying *real* hard to push her away, Ace," I say sarcastically.

We're both panting in anger; our faces are red. The sun beating down on my back is making my body burn even more. Our eyes are still locked, both of us pushing pure hate through our gazes at the moment. Love is completely forgotten, and rage and pain are in its place.

"I suggest you leave before I say something I regret," Ace vows.

I bite my bottom lip to stop the sob that is fighting tooth and nail to break out. My heart is shattering into a million pieces, because I took a risk on this man and he didn't care, love or respect me enough to end things with me first before he moved on to the next woman.

I step up to the car, giving Ace my back. I pull the door open and take one last look at the man who held my heart and then squeezed the life out of it.

"I already regret it," I mutter, knowing he heard me because he sucks in a harsh breath. I climb into my car and close the door before starting the engine and pulling away from the clubhouse.

I have no idea how I drove home. I was supposed to go back to the café, but I couldn't go back there. I can never step foot inside there again. It holds too many good memories for me. Staying as far away from the cafe and anything thing to do with Ace and the club is the best thing for me to do.

I walk straight to my bedroom and close the door behind me. I climb into my bed, not bothering to undress. I feel completely numb. My phone rings, and I squeeze my eyes shut, hoping it stops. I pull the covers over my head, shutting out the world. I'll start planning tomorrow. Right now, I want to sleep.

My phone dings with a text message. I reach for it, in the small pocket of my dress. I see Zarah's name and my lungs push out the breath I was holding, but my heart hurts at the same time. I'm glad it's her and not him, but I'm sad because it reminds me that I'm leaving her or forcing her to come with me.

Zarah: You coming back to the cafe, or has your man got you tied to his bed, doing wicked things to you? ;)

Me: I'm home. Not feeling very well. I'll see you tonight. I'm going to get some sleep.

Zarah: You okay? Do I need to come to you?

Me: No! Stay there. I'm going to sleep.

Zarah: Okay, Smallie. I'll catch you later. Love you.

Me: Love you too.

I turn my phone off and slide it under the pillow. I catch a whiff of Ace's scent, and my chest caves as I let out a violent sob.

My chest feels like it's being crushed. I fling the pillow across the room.

I cry for hours, running through our moments together, but then the scene I walked in on ruins all the happy times. We haven't been together long, but we knew it was coming. I don't understand how he can put so much effort into chasing me, just to throw it all away. But I saw what I saw. He was going to have sex with her, wasn't he? I mean she was naked and had her boobs in his face. And he was *not* pushing her away.

I shake my head and grip the blanket around me tighter. I want to melt into my bed, so no one can find me. I just need me time. Time to sort through all the images flashing through my brain.

———

I wake with start when I hear the front door slam shut.

"Smallie, where are you?" Zarah's voice comes through the house.

"Bedroom," I say, but the words get caught in my throat. I cough and try again. "Bedroom, Z," I say louder, hoping she hears me. I hear her running up the stairs and my bedroom door opening.

"Oh, Smallie." The emotion in her voice makes me crack again. I cry into my pillow. The blanket lifts and the bed dips as my sister climbs into the bed with me. I get wrapped up in her arms and held as I cry. Zarah tightens her grip on me and I hear her sniff. She is crying for me. That is why we are so close: we always have each other's back, and we hurt together.

"How did you know?"

"EC called and told me to check on you. I forced it out of him —what happened. He said Ace teared the bar apart after you left and kicked Clover out of the club."

"Too late," I mutter against her chest.

"I know, Smallie." We stay silent for some time, just lying under the covers. My crying has stopped. My face feels puffy and sore from crying so hard.

"I need to leave." Zarah jerks her body away from mine and glares at me with a fierce look in her eyes.

"Hell fucking no. You are stronger than this. I will not have another man run you out of your home." The blankets are thrown off us and she sits up and stares down at me. "This is your home. The cafe is yours. Ace can take a long jump off a short cliff if he thinks he will run you out of town." She takes a deep breath and climbs from the bed, before walking out of my bedroom. I frown at her leaving, but she's back within seconds with a cold wash cloth and lays it over my face.

The coolness sinks into my skin, feeling bloody amazing. "Oh, that feels nice," I mutter under the cloth.

"You look like the elephant man after all that crying." I smile, but I know she can't see me.

"Thanks, Z. For the record, I don't think he will run me out of town. Avoid me, yeah. But he knows how much I love the cafe and how much Nancy wanted me to run it."

"Okay, I will give you that, but if he gives you any shit, I will go Kung Fu Panda on his arse. Got it?" I nod.

"Ice cream. Chocolate. Nik Naks. Alcohol. All are needed tonight," Zarah says, walking out of the room. "Come out when you're ready." I let out a big breath and take the face cloth off my face, dropping it on the floor next to the bed.

Climbing out of my bed, I pull my dress up and over my head, before dropping that to the floor as well. I take off my bra and walk over to my dresser and pull out some cool pyjamas. I pick my teal and leopard set. The cami is teal with a lace trim and the shorts are leopard print with a teal lace trim.

I pick up a hair-tie and put my hair up in a messy bun and walk out into the living room to see my sister already on the couch with the coffee table filled with all our favourite junk foods.

"Come on, Smallie. We need to pick some sexy thing to watch." She wiggles her eyebrows at me, and I smile at her.

"Okay, so who are we watching tonight? No SOA, please?" I joke, but my heart hurts. I can't handle biker tonight, even though we love Charlie Hunnam.

"Okay, since no bikers but we love Charlie, how about some *Pacific Rim*?"

"Deal." We settle in and watch the film, stuffing our faces with as much junk as we can without being sick. After *Pacific Rim*, we watch a *The Shallows* because I love sharks.

Thanks to Zarah, the films and the junk food—which believe me, helps—I forget about Ace and my heartbreak for a short time. But once I'm in bed again, the pain and hurt comes rushing back. I cry myself to sleep, thinking of how I'm going to live without Ace McGowan in my life.

Ace

YESTERDAY WAS THE WORST FUCKING DAY OF MY LIFE. CLOVER coming into my office and causing shit was the final straw for her. I wanted to see how far she would take things, but that backfired when Ana walked in on us. She thought the worst of me. The hurt and pain in her eyes will haunt for the rest of the days we are apart.

Fighting with her in the courtyard was fucking brutal. I have never been so angry at a woman as I was with her yesterday, and I know some of that anger stemmed from Clover's bullshit moves. I needed a reason to kick Clover out of the club. It's in the bylaws of the club that a club girl needs to make a threat against a patched member or his old lady and thank fuck Clover did that yesterday.

She offered to take out Ana, make sure she never comes around the club again, and guess who she used? The fucking suits. I was smiling at her, thinking about the perfect words to tell her she was done with the club, when my woman opened the fucking door and took everything the wrong way.

Once Ana said her final words to me yesterday—*I already regret it*—my world crumbled. My chest caved, and my heart stopped.

I walked into the clubhouse like a fucking zombie, dead on my feet, until Clover stepped into the room, and some of my brothers followed me in. She was smiling, looking like a triumphant troll with her overly-done-up face and hair.

"I told you she can't handle the club life. You're better off without her," she said to me in front of the boys. That's when all I saw was red. I lunged for her, but Court and Batch got to me first, seeing the rage in my eyes.

"YOU FUCKING CUNT." I had tried getting to her again, but my brothers weren't letting me go. Suede and Lola had come running into the room and asked what was happening. How I managed to explain is beyond me, but I did. Lola walked over to Clover and floored the bitch with one punch.

Suede banned her from the club for life and ordered her out that minute. Lola had followed her to make sure she packed only her shit and left.

Once they were out of the room, the boys let me go, but the rage was still burning inside of me. I picked up the closest chair and slammed it against the table, watching as it shattered into pieces.

The raging animal in me broke, and nothing was safe from me. I smashed up a few chairs and tables, and I overturned the sofa. The boys let me rage, but then Suede put a stop to it, ordering Dyson to take me to my room to calm my arse down with a bottle of gin. I drank myself stupid to stop myself from going to Ana and begging her to talk to me.

Which brings us to now at eleven o'clock in the morning with me laying my head on the bar, a stampede in my skull.

"Hair of the dog, brother." Bear hands be a bottle of beer.

"Fuck, I need sleep—maybe spew my guts up, then sleep. Fuck, don't ever let me drink like that again," I say to anyone who will listen. I hate—fucking hate—getting drunk. I hate not having control over my senses.

"Drink some water or Lucozade then and take some

painkillers. That should help." He chuckles. "Get one of the club girls to make you a fry-up, that will soak the alcohol." My stomach rolls at the thought of food, but I know he's right.

"Oh shit." I bolt off the bar stool and run to the toilet, just making it in time. I spew the drink back up from last night, completely emptying my stomach. Oh God, fucking kill me now. I lean on the porcelain bowl and take a deep breath, but the stench of the acid and the gin make me retch again.

"You okay, man?" Dyson asks from behind me. I fall back against the wall, resting my head back, looking up at the tiled ceiling.

"I'm dying, brother." The bastard chuckles. Yeah, I'll remember that, fuckhead. He kicks my foot before speaking.

"Come on, we have church."

"Fuck, can't I die in peace?"

"You can't die at all, man. Come on." He holds his hand out to me, and I take it and let him drag me to my feet. "Let's get this shit sorted."

"She wants nothing to do with me." I step up to the sink and splash some water over my face, before drinking some, swilling it around my mouth and spitting it out.

"Give her time. Let's go before Prez sends out a search party for us." I take a deep breath and follow behind him. The room is deathly quiet. The boys give me a sympathetic nod.

Suede bangs the gavel and it vibrates through my head. I wince and rest my elbows on the table and my head in my hands.

"Sorry, brother." I nod but don't look up. "The plan is set to go down tonight. Everything is in place, thanks to Ace and Click."

"She isn't coming, is she?" EC pipes up.

"Do you really think I would put her in danger, brother?" My head lifts at the tone in Suede's voice.

"No, but I know how fucking stubborn she is."

Suede speaks up. "Get her in here."

"Wait. What?" EC is sputtering as the door opens and Click

walks in, dressed like a man's wet dream. Did I forget to mention that Click is a fucking stunner? Tall for her age. Her chocolate brown hair down her back, big green innocent eyes, and the perfect set of lips a man could wish for—well, except for me because my Ana is a fucking knock out.

Click may be a geek or a nerd, but she is beautiful. EC's mouth drops open as she saunters into the room with her laptop open and resting on her arm.

Maze goes to stand to give her his seat, but EC growls, making Click roll her eyes.

"I'll stand, but thanks, Maze." Oh, the girl is trouble, but I know she wants EC just as much as he wants her. But the history there is fucked up.

"I've tracked where the dicks go most of the day. They seem to have a pattern, and thanks to EC planting the tracker, we can see where they go. They only go to these three locations." EC puffs out his chest when she says he did a good job. Good little pretty boy.

"These are the times they're there." She hands me a sheet of paper with times and durations they are there for. I look over the numbers and see the pattern clear as day.

"I say we hit tonight at ten. They seem to be there for the longest time then, settling in for the night."

"Why the fuck are they staying there?" asks Batch.

"No clue, brother, but we strike tonight. Thanks, darlin'." I look at Click, and she blushes a little and closes her laptop. She walks up to me with her laptop tucked under her arm and leans in to whisper in my ear. My eyes go straight to EC, who is slaughtering me in his head for having his woman this close to me.

"For what it's worth, she's looking like shit too—heartbroken. Fix it."

I nod and watch as she leaves the room.

"What the fuck was that?" EC growls from across the table.

"None of your fucking business, brother." I wink at him and he charges to his feet, making everyone laugh.

"Don't push me when it comes to her, Ace. Just because you fucked up with Mouse, doesn't mean you can make a move on the one woman I want." That sets my anger boiling again. I slam my chair back and stand.

"Watch what the fuck you're saying, boy."

"Why? If you make move on Mae, then for-fucking-sure I'm going to make a move on Ana." He smirks at me, thinking he has me. I lunge across the table and land a solid punch to his jaw. He tries to throw a punch back at me, but I'm quicker. I'm not the Sergeant-at-Arms for nothing.

"Enough," Suede bellows. Dyson pulls me off EC and Batch pulls EC to his feet. "Grow the fuck up, will you. We got shit to get done." I give EC the middle finger and take my seat while we go over the plans for tonight.

We're all spread out around the warehouse. Suede wanted me to pull in my brother, Solar's, MC, but I told him we could handle it on our own. Dyson and I are close to the front, waiting for the fucking suits to arrive. We need to get the girls out with minimal bloodshed to them, but I want these wankers dead and fucking buried.

It doesn't take long before they arrive, walking around their car like they're kings of the fucking world. We wait for the word from Suede to go all in.

"Go. Go. Go." Suede voice comes through our earpieces. We jump to our feet and storm the place, not giving them time to react. Maze and EC's jobs are to get the girls we know are being held in one of the small back rooms. My gun is drawn, and I take down the man who is sitting on a chair. He topples over, but I'm moving on before he even hits the floor.

Pain hits my bicep and I duck behind a wall. I look down and see blood seeping into my shirt, but it looks like a graze. I grit my teeth and move to the next room. The girls scream, and I can only hope it's because of the gunfire.

"Fuck," I hear being screamed. "I'm hit." Maze.

"How bad?" I yell over the noise.

"My fucking shoulder." I try to make my way to Maze when I come face to face with one of the suits. He has a girl in front on him, using her as a shield.

"You're okay, sweetheart. We'll get you out of this."

"Clear," I hear from somewhere. I smile at him, and he just smirks back at me. He doesn't fear death, that is clear.

"Give up, pal. You ain't getting out of here."

"You think?"

"I do. Hand the girl over and we can talk this shit out." He knows I'm lying, but I have to try.

"Not happening. I know how this shit works. You let me go and I won't hurt her."

"Now who's lying, you son of a bitch. You killed Eliza. And for what?" I demand.

"You tainted what was mine. I need payback."

"What the fuck are you talking about? I haven't touched anything of yours."

"I believe you have. Multiple times. She tastes fucking good, doesn't she." He smirks at me like I should know who the fuck he's talking about. "Does she still flush all the way up from her tits to her neck when she comes?"

My breath catches in my throat. Ana—he's talking about Ana. How does he know her?

"I see the wheels turning, and you worked it out. Ana is my wife, you twat."

Wife? No way, she would have told me. Fuck, no, she wouldn't have. She hasn't told me fuck all about her past. He takes the split-second advantage and fires at me, hitting me in the stomach. I fall back to the ground, hearing the girl's screams.

I feel pressure on my body. I force my eyes open and see the girl putting pressure on my wound. The fucker shot me. *Holy fuck.*

"Help! In here. He's been shot," she screams, tears running down her face. I lay there, flashes of the club, my mum, and Ana flickering behind my closed eyes. I reach up and touch the girl's hand on my lower body.

"Tell Ana I love her, and that I'm sorry." I know she has no fucking clue who I'm talking about, but I needed to say it.

"Stay with us, brother. Fuck me, Ana will kick my arse if something happens to you." My eyes flutter open and I see EC kneeling over me.

"Love her," I whisper, before everything turns cold and black.

Ana

I TOSS AND TURN IN BED, MY STOMACH NOT SETTLING AT ALL TODAY. I give up. I climb out of bed and go to the kitchen to make myself a cup of tea. Hopefully that will help—and maybe some toast.

The kettle is almost boiled when—

Bang. Bang. Bang.

Someone comes banging on my front door. I shriek, almost dropping the spoon in my hand. I place my other hand over my chest to calm my beating heart.

"What the hell?" Zarah says, coming down the stairs. I shake my head.

"Ana, open the door." Maze's voice comes through the door. My heart sinks, and Zarah is there by my side. I place my hands over my stomach.

"Ace," I whisper. Zarah kisses the side of my head before walking over to open the door to Maze. I slowly move towards him, and I see his face. Oh no. My hand flies to my mouth as I shake my head.

"Ace has been hurt, babe. You need to come to the hospital." I'm frozen to the spot.

"He is dead?"

"No. Hurt—badly," Maze replies.

I feel arms wrap around me and pull me up the stairs.

"Come on, let's get you dressed, and then we can go and see Ace, okay?" I stand there and watch as my sister pulls clothes out for me and puts them on the bed. I feel numb. I don't even know if I'm crying.

Zarah appears in front of me. She grips my shoulders and tells me to get dressed. I listen and take off my pyjamas, before sliding on my jeans and a loose vest. I don't bother with a bra. Flip flops get dropped at my feet, so I put them on, and then I'm being tugged back down the stairs to a waiting Maze, who tucks his phone away when he sees us.

"Come on, Mouse. Let's take you to see your man." I cringe at the words, because he isn't my man anymore.

In a flash we're at the hospital. The lift doors open, and I see all the brothers sitting in the chairs around the room. Suede is pacing. I see EC in the corner of the room, covered in blood. He looks at me, offers me a sad smile, before turning to look out the window next to him. The room is sullen. Everyone is feeling the pain of Ace being hurt.

"Ana." I look at Suede. "He's okay, and awake. Dyson is in with him. You can go in." I shake my head, but he insists. "He wants to see you."

He takes my hand and leads me to the room. My heart has now kicked into high gear and is trying its best to break through my chest. Suede pushes the door open to a private room.

I gasp when I see Ace sitting up in bed with a large dressing over his lower stomach. My hand covers my mouth, and both Ace and Dyson look in our direction.

"Baby." Ace's voice is hoarse. I can only assume from the tube they had down his throat when they operated. Maze explained to us in the car what had happened.

I walk over to the bed, tucking my hands in the back pockets of my jeans to stop myself from reaching out to him.

"Come here, babe. I need to feel you." I shake my head. I understand he's hurt, but the picture of them together still rules my thoughts.

"Ana, please, baby." His voice cracks with emotion, and that alone breaks my restraint. I lean over him, wrapping my arms around his neck, sobbing into his body.

"I'm okay, baby. I swear I am. I'm so fucking sorry for everything that's happened. Please tell me you forgive me." I nod against his neck. "Words, baby; I need words."

"I forgive you," I breath out between sobs. I lift my head and our eyes meet.

"Baby, I didn't touch her. It was a set-up, and she failed. She's gone—out of the club." I nod.

"Okay," I whisper. "I believe you." He kisses my lips softly, like a butterfly's touch.

"God, I missed you. I thought I would never see you again, and as much as that makes me sound like a pussy, I don't fucking care." I nod and smile at him. My first smile in days. His face gets serious, and he takes my cheeks in his hand.

"We need to talk. I know you hate talking about your past, but I'm sorry, baby, it's come into our present." I frown at him, not having a clue what he's talking about.

"Gary Molloy," is all he says. My heart stops and my body runs cold. I try to pull out of his arms, but his grip tightens. He winces as his muscles tighten around me.

"No." I pull harder, and he lets me go. I can't go far though, as Dyson and Suede are blocking the door.

"Baby girl, you're going to have to explain. He's caused the club some shit over the last few weeks." I gasp, and it all comes flooding back to me. The news of the girls being attacked, the men in suits... Oh my God, Gary killed Eliza.

"Start at the beginning," Ace says. I take a deep breath and go to stand by the window. I knew this day would come—when I would have to explain my past.

"I married Gary young. I was stupid and in love. Not long after we got married, I fell pregnant. But I lost..." A sob bubbles up from my throat before I can stop it. I'm lifted off my feet and placed on the bed next to Ace, who gingerly wraps one arm around me, taking my hand in the other.

"Carry on, baby. I've got you."

"I lost the baby at thirteen weeks. After that, Gary became abusive, both mentally and physically. Twice he put me in the hospital. He's high up in the crime world, so I didn't see the point is pressing charges. He gets away with everything. Zarah helped me leave and file for divorce. It was a friend's address we used, so he couldn't contact me. It got messy for a while, but we got there, and I was granted a divorce."

I wipe the tears away and sit up, so I can face Ace. "I wish I was stronger then, but I wasn't. Zarah helped me out the last time he hurt me bad. She dropped everything, and we moved around until we landed here."

"And I'm so fucking happy that you did, baby, because I've got you now, and no fucker will hurt you."

I nod, feeling my chest starting to relax. "He's the one who attacked the girls, isn't he?" I look between the three men, each of them nodding. "That bastard." My head snaps to Ace. "He shot you?"

"Yeah, baby. We were rescuing some girls he was holding. He told me about you, and then he took a shot while I was processing." I gasp and jump from the bed again.

"You got shot because of me," I state, my hands shaking. Oh God, no.

"Yeah, babe. You brought a shit load of trouble into the club that we didn't fucking need. You should have kept your legs closed and away from the fucking club." I spin around at the sound of the voice.

I see Court scowling at me, like he wants to string me up. I didn't notice some of the boys had come into the room.

Dyson turns around in a flash and punches Court in the stomach, and then they start to fight against the wall.

"Stop," I scream. I sob into my hands because what he said is right. I brought trouble into the club and didn't tell them, and now Ace is recovering from a gunshot wound.

"Prez, I swear to fucking Christ you had better get that fucker out of here before I slit his fucking throat for speaking to my girl like that," Ace growls. A nurse comes running into the room and stops in her tracks when she sees the boys in leather.

"Everyone out, now. Visiting hours are over and he needs his rest." She stands with her hands on her hips, showing no fear. I look at Ace and then the door. I take a step forward, but before I can take another, his voice stops me.

"Take one more step and I will put you over my knee, babe. Get your sexy arse over here. My woman is staying," he adds to the nurse. I'm frozen in place again, my eyes bouncing between him and the boys in the room. They're smirking at me. Suede winks and leaves the room after saying he'll be back in the morning.

"You alright, brother?" Dyson asks Ace. He nods, never taking his eyes off me. I sigh and walk over to the chair in the corner. The brothers file out, leaving us alone in the now quiet hospital room.

"Come here," he demands. I shake my head, trying to clear the thoughts that are racing around the track in my head. Ace sighs and lays his head back against the pillow.

"I'm sorry. I did this," I mutter, sitting in the chair. He doesn't look at me, just keeps his head back and his eyes closed. He's never going to forgive me for causing so much trouble for the club. The weight of what I've done is crushing. I try to pull air into my lungs but it's getting harder and harder. A black cloud starts blurring my vision, and I struggle to breathe.

I feel soft hands on my wrists, making me lift my head. I see the nurse from earlier, smiling at me.

"Slow breaths in and slow breaths out. In and out. Good girl." Her smile is reassuring, and I begin to breathe normally. "There you go. A few more, that's it." I listen to her voice, it's a calming and soothing tone. It must be a nurse tone.

"Is she okay?" comes a gruff voice from the bed.

"I think she'll be fine, looks like a panic attack," the nurse explains. "Does this happen a lot?" I shake my head.

"Not anymore," I whisper. She smiles at me and leaves the room after checking on Ace's machines.

The silence is deafening. I play with the hem of my camisole, waiting for him to say something. I can't find the words to speak. I feel like I'll say the wrong thing at any moment.

"Ana, I—"

"It's okay. I'll go. I understand." I thought the pain I felt was bad when I saw him with Clover, but this... this pain is damned near killing me. I know I won't ever survive without him. I slowly walk towards the door, dragging my heavy body away from the man I love.

"Ana, just stop." I stop and brace my hand on the wall, before turning my head to look at him. He has tears in his eyes, and it causes my heart to crack that little bit more. I hate seeing men cry.

"Come here, please." I shake my head. I know me touching him will turn me to putty in his hands. "Please, babe."

I squeeze my eyes shut tight, so tight I see white flashes behind my eyelids. I slowly turn to face him but keep my head down. I take one step, then two, towards the bed.

He speaks first. "Baby, you are not to blame for any of the shit that's happened. *He is.*" He growls the last two words. "We're going to be fine. I'm going to be fine. We start new, from now, do you hear me?" I shake my head. "Yes. Ace and Ana from the start. Nothing and no one will stop us from being together, including us."

"Too much has been said and done, Ace."

"But we're strong enough to push it all away. Always."

He reaches for my hand and winces from the pain. No doubt pulling the stitches he has in his stomach.

"Careful, honey." I step right up to the bed, so he doesn't have to stretch.

A smile crosses his face, and he lifts my hand to kiss my knuckles.

"I've missed you calling me that." He kisses my hand again, and I smile at him.

"Can we truly get past this?"

"Hell yeah, we can, babe. Come and lay with me."

"No, Ace, I'll hurt you."

"You could never hurt me, baby. Come here." I gently climb onto the bed, careful of the wires and his wound. He wraps an arm around my shoulders, holding me to him. Then he pulls one of my legs over his thighs, holding me trapped there. I rest one of my hands on his chest.

My heart starts to beat to the same rhythm as Ace's, and it's then I believe that we will be okay. We will get past this.

"Is she really gone?" I don't need to say her name; he knows who I'm talking about.

"Yeah, baby. She is gone for good. The rest of the club girls have been warned." I nod.

"And Gary?"

"He got away. When he shot me, he threw the girl and legged it. We'll find him, babe."

"Are the girls okay?"

"Typical Ana, always looking out for others. Yeah, sweetheart, they're all okay, and are home." I sigh and snuggle into him more, loving the feel of his warm skin against mine.

We sleep together—well, the best we can in between the nurses coming to check on my man.

My man. Ace McGowan is my man again. I smile and fall asleep again. Hoping tomorrow brings a better day.

Ana

THANK THE LORD FOR CLICK, AKA MAE, BUT ALSO CURSE HER FOR her beauty. She has been a Godsend, coming here to help in the café, but because of her, our customers have almost tripled in numbers.

It's been three weeks since Ace got shot. The club and Click are still trying to track down Gary, but they aren't getting anywhere.

I hear giggling from the front table and look up to see Mae standing there talking to a table full of boys, all around her age. I smile at the young ones enjoying life. I'm loving life right now; everyone seems happy and living for the day.

My phone dings in my dress pocket. I pull it out and smile when I see Ace's name. I slide the bar across the screen and read what he sent me.

Ace: I can't stop thinking about you.

Me: Ditto, honey.

Ace: I can still smell you on me.

Oh God. I can feel my blush creeping up my neck. He woke me up this morning with his head between my legs. He made me come twice before he slid inside of me. That man has such a talented tongue. Ace likes to make sure I come before him. Even when I decide to give him a blowjob, he always turns me around so we're doing a sixty-nine position. He loves my mouth on him, but he loves to make me come more. Strange man, but hey, who am I to complain.

Me: You are making me blush, Mr. McGowan.

Ace: I love seeing you blush, babe.

Me: Are you coming by the cafe to see me today?

Ace: Yeah, baby, will be there soon.

I turn to go back to the kitchen. I need to sort out the sandwiches for the lovely older couple who are in town visiting their son and his baby. The back screen door is open, and I know I didn't open it because of flies and other bugs getting in. We open the main door but leave the screen door shut in the hot weather.

I'm moving over to close it when a large hand tugs hard on my wrist, yanking me out through the door. I go to scream, but I'm hit over the head and everything goes black.

When I come to, the first thing I notice is the pain. I cry out. I hurt all over my body. I try to open my eyes but my left one seems swollen shut. Who hit me? Then his voice startles me and brings the old fear to the forefront of my mind and body.

"Oh look, the cunt is awake." I try to coil back from his voice above me, but I'm tied to the bed. My arms and ankles are stretched and tied to the four posts of the bed. A slap crosses my face when I don't look at him. It was one of the things Gary hated; he always like to look me in the eyes when he beat me.

"Why?" I whisper.

"Why? Why, you ask? Well, let me tell you, you little bitch. You left me after I gave you fucking everything. And you couldn't even carry a fucking baby. Something millions of women have been doing for thousands of years, and you couldn't do the simple job of carrying my child. Fucking useless bitch." His fist connects with my ribs, and I scream out in pain, making him and other people in the room laugh.

Ace's face flashes in my head, his words of strength floating around my head.

You are stronger than you look, baby. Women were put on this planet to help it grow and flourish. So fucking grow, get strong, and flourish the fuck out of life.

I can't stop the smile from creeping across my face, nor the laugh that bubbles up. The pain subsides as I think of the man that holds my heart.

"What the fuck are you smiling and laughing about?" He slaps me again, making me laugh even louder. I can't stop. I sound like a fucking maniac.

"You say that I'm weak for not carrying your baby, but you are the weak man for hitting a woman who could never defend herself against you. I would love to see you and Ace—or any of the brothers of the Unforgiven Riders—get into a boxing ring together. Then we'd see who the real man is. And, my darling Gary, it will *never* be you."

I feel the first punch, and the second, but after that I go numb, my brain shutting down and blocking out the pain.

The hits finally stop, and I'm left alone. Thank God for small mercies. I have no clue how long I've been here.

I think of how the boys are. I bet Ace and Zarah are going frantic trying to find me, because I know they will find me. I have complete faith in the club; in Click. I fall asleep, but no clue for how long.

The door opens with a bang, startling me awake.

"Oh, my dear Ana, how shitty you are looking."

"Thanks," I mutter through my swollen lips. The taste of blood lingers on my tongue.

"When did you become such a smart mouth, sweetie? You were never this mouthy with me. I take it your new man can't control you, huh?"

I think of a smart comeback, but I know it will end in more hits. I hear hurried footsteps, and then his hand is gripping my jaw, squeezing it tightly, to the point of pain, and making my sore slips push together.

"Fucking answer me," he bellows in my face. I try to turn my head, but he slaps me again. He slams my head down against the mattress and covers my mouth and nose with his hand, cutting off my air. I struggle, thrashing my head back and forth, but he isn't letting me go. Black dots appear in the vision of my right eye, before everything turns black.

When I wake up next, I'm hanging from the beams by metal chains, my toes scraping the ground. My shoulders ache—I'm pretty sure my right shoulder is dislocated.

I'm naked, except for my underwear. I mentally check that he's only hit me and not raped me, but I feel nothing bad down there. I sigh and pray it stays that way. He raped me twice when we were together, and that last time was the final straw for me.

I try to calculate my injures, but I hurt everywhere. There's no telling how much damage he's caused me. My hope of the club finding me is fading. I don't know how long I've been here; the room has no windows and he keeps knocking me out. All I can do is hope and pray they come for me. I dread to think how Ace will cope with losing me. It's probably the same way I would feel if I ever lost him.

The door opens again, and my body jerks out of fear, making Gary and his two henchmen laugh. They look smug, and all I can think of is how I would love to see one of the brothers wipe it off their faces.

"Oh look, she's awake again. You do sleep a lot these days, Ana Banana." He chuckles. Now you see why I loathe that nickname.

"You are going to die soon, Gary. I can promise you that."

"If you say so, sweetie. But have that grubby little club come for you yet? Huh? Sorry I can't hear you... No." I close my eyes and will the tears to stay back, but I fail. I cry... I cry for Ace and me. For Zarah.

"Oh, she's crying, boss. Maybe I could give her something to cry about," one of the men says. My fear spikes because I don't know how these different men act. I watch out of my eyes as he walks towards me. He removes his suit jacket and starts to roll the sleeves up.

I whimper, and he smiles a sadistic smile at me, before the first punch catches my bottom ribs. The pain tears through me as the bone cracks. I scream and scream as he uses me like a human punching bag.

"STOP!" I scream, sobbing through the pain. I wish for numbness or death at this moment.

"Please, stop." I'm panting, trying to control my breathing so I don't pass out.

"But we're just getting started, Ana. My boys need to have their fun too. This is what you get for running from me and sleeping with that disgusting criminal. Opening your legs for him, giving him something that belongs to me. Which is why I took something of his." He smirks at me. At one point in my life, I loved that smirk. Now, it turns my stomach.

I cough and vomit. Lucky for me, it catches the second man as he steps up to me.

I get a slap and my hair pulled for that. He rips my head back by my hair, making me cry out again.

"You think you're funny, cunt? I'll show you funny." He steps from me and yanks on the chains, causing the metal around my wrist to jerk. I scream as the pain sears through my shoulders. He hauls me up so I'm high off the ground, and I hang there, with my life in his hands as he holds the chain.

I hear the first gunshot, and my heart jumps in my chest. *Please let that be Ace and the brothers,* I pray over and over again in my head.

The metal door springs open, and the brothers flood into the room, guns drawn. Ace runs in my direction, but as he gets closer, the man holding the chains lets go. I fall to the floor, seeing the horror on Ace's face as I hit the concrete. My head bounces off the surface, and everything goes from blurry to black. The last thing I hear is Ace, calling my name.

Ace

YOU REMEMBER WHEN I SAID MY FIGHT WITH ANA AT THE clubhouse was the worst day of my life? Yeah, I fucking lied. This is. This one fucking day. I got the phone call as I was turning onto the street of the cafe. It was Ditch telling me Ana was gone.

Taken.

Taken from me.

We searched for hours for them. We had every man on the job looking, but we were all coming up empty. Then Click came running into the clubhouse with a friend of hers from college, and together they were able to track down Gary and his men, and where they took Ana. EC wasn't overly happy to see Click there with another bloke, but it wasn't the time to deal with that shit.

We drove to the location Click found, and true to her search, they were there. The two big BMW SUV's a sure sign. We parked away from the building, making sure they didn't hear us coming. Again, using Suede's favourite strategy, we storm the place, guns blazing. Thank fuck Click's friend was able to check how many men were in there by checking surrounding cameras.

We took out each man, and then we heard the scream.

Now, I'm running like my life depends on it—fuck, it does depend on it. Court kicks the door in and shots get fired. I don't take notice of my brothers; my focus is on Ana, who is suspended by chains from the high beams. The fucker holding the end of the chain laughs a manic laugh before letting the chain go, and I watch is absolute horror as Ana drops to the floor. Her near naked body is like a ragdoll as it hits solid ground. Her head bounces off the concrete, and I scream her name.

"ANA!"

I aim my gun at the dick who dropped her, and my bullet hits him square in the chest. He stumbles back, but I don't see him hit the ground as I'm sliding to floor next to Ana.

"Ana, baby, talk to me. Wake up."

"Clear." I hear from around me. I brush her hair off her face, blood matted in the strands. Her face is swollen to the point where she's almost unrecognisable. My poor baby. My always.

I growl as I pull her body to me. I bury my face in her neck, not bothered about her blood seeping into my clothes.

I've lost her.

My girl is gone.

"Ace, move," Bull growls from my side. But I shake my head and hold my baby tighter to me. I feel arms slide under mine and pull me away as Bull eases Ana's body to the floor. I bellow and kick at everyone around me.

"Let me get to her. She needs me." Dyson's face appears in front of me. He holds my head so that we're eye to eye.

"Let Bull check her over. An ambulance is on its way. Horton has been called. He'll back us up. He knows the story, okay?" I nod, forcing my head from his hand, and crawl over to Ana. She looks so broken.

"She's alive, Ace. She's a strong girl; she *will* pull through this. She has a shit load of injuries, but it's her head injury I'm worried about," Bull explains.

I brush back the hair from her forehead and kiss her face.

"You have to stay with me, baby. I can't live without you. You're my life, my air. I need you, Ana. Flourish, baby. Always." I cry, not giving a fuck if my brothers are around me. I'm man enough to admit my feelings, especially where Ana is concerned.

"Baby, please?" I sob, resting my head on top of hers. I hear the sirens, but I don't move. I need to be close to her, touching her. I keep my eyes on her beaten face, remembering how she looks, because I know this will fuel my anger when I find that cocksucker Gary. I kiss her lips when I hear a flurry of footsteps.

"Sir, step aside so we can get ready to transport her the hospital. What's her name?" I slide to the side, but not too far away.

"Ana. I'm staying here. She's my woman," I grumble. I wipe the tears away, then place my hand on her head again, keeping one of her hands locked in mine.

"Son, let them work," Suede says from behind me, clutching my shoulder. I take a deep breath and nod. I watch as they check her over, trying to get a response out of her but getting nothing. My hope of her pulling through this is fading. They put a needle in her hand, for fuck knows what, but I have to trust they know what they're doing. Bull is just as close as I am, making sure they're treating her the right way. Bull is an ex-army medic.

"Let's move," one of the paramedics says—I have no clue which one. I watch as they lift her onto the stretcher before checking over more things on her body, then we are moving outside. I see each of my brothers lining a path to the ambulance. My heart feels full of love for my brothers for always having my back, and at the same time it aches for my girl.

"We'll follow behind you," Dyson says, and I give him a nod. They load Ana into the back of the ambulance and I climb in after them. Suede gives me a sympathetic smile before he closes the door and taps it for good measure.

The drive to the hospital drags like you wouldn't believe. Ana seems stable, according to her heart monitor. The guy in the back with us ask questions about Ana which I answer, but I scowl at him when he asks about what happened

We arrive at the hospital and the first thing I hear are the sounds of my brothers' bikes parking up. I climb out of the ambulance and they unload Ana and rush her through the double doors, but I'm stopped by a nurse.

"You can't go back there, honey. Someone will come and get you when they have news."

"But she's my woman; I need to be with her," I half growl, half sob. She pats my arms, offering some sort of comfort.

"I know, hun. I'll be back as soon as I can, okay?" I have no choice but to nod.

I fall against the wall and slide down to the floor, the emotion taking over. I sob like a fucking baby. I feel like a failure for letting her down, for letting her get taken by that cunt.

Arms come around my shoulders, pulling me into a hard body. I don't need to look up to know it's Dyson. He sits with me on the floor for fuck knows how long. Time passes in a blur.

Suede pops in to tell me all the brothers and some of the old ladies are in the waiting room, with Zarah. Oh fuck—Zarah... I had completely forgotten about her.

I climb to my feet and make my way to the other important person is Ana's life. When I push the door open, Zarah runs at me. I hold her tight, whispering words of comfort that I hope like fuck come true.

I hold her to my chest and lift my head to look around the room. Every one of my brothers are here, including my blood brother, Solar. My resolve breaks again seeing him here. Zarah steps back and Solar grips me in a bear hug, holding me tight to him. I cry, letting it all out again. My brother, who drove fucking hours to be here with me while I wait to find out what is happening to my girl.

"I thought you would want him here," EC speaks up. I nod in gratitude.

"Thanks, brother."

"Any news?" Solar asks. I shake my head.

"Nothing."

"She's strong, Ace. She will pull through," Zarah adds. I wrap my arms around her shoulders, holding her to me. She needs me as much as I need her. We both love Ana.

The door opens and a doctor walks in, followed by the nurse who stopped me earlier. I still have no idea how much time has passed, but it must be hours if Solar is here.

"Family of Ana Molloy?"

"Dawkins," I growl out.

"She's divorced. Changed her name," Zarah explains when the doctor looks at the file in his hand. He nods his understanding as Sully walks in through the door. Sully is the second-generation club doctor.

"Ana is stable—that is the good news. She's suffered a dislocated shoulder and three broken ribs. They will heal, so will the cuts and bruises she sustained from the attack. Our main concern is her head injury. Ana suffered an injury to her frontal lobe, which will affect her movement, behaviour, and memory."

"So she won't remember me—us?" I question. He sighs and goes to speak, but Sully speaks first.

"We won't know anything until she wakes up, Ace. At the moment, Ana is in an induced coma to help her heal. Rest is the best thing for her. We'll give her a few days to recover before we bring her out of the coma, okay."

"Not okay, Sul. I need her to be okay. I can't fucking lose her."

"And you won't," Solar says from my side.

"Let her heal, and we will go from there," the doc says. I nod, again the option taken from me.

"You can go and see her, but one at a time."

"No, me and her sister need to see her together," I demand.

The doctor doesn't look happy, but Sully whispers in his ear. His cheeks flush a little and he nods. Sully winks at me, and then we are led down the hall. I make sure I keep Zarah's hand tight in mine.

The first thing I see are the machines. They're everywhere. I drop my gaze to Ana sleeping in the bed, looking tiny. Zarah leaves my side and goes to her sister. I pinch my lips together to stop the sob that's trying to break free. I need to stay strong for my woman.

"Oh, Ace." Zarah whimpers my name. I walk over to the bed and take one of Ana's hands in mine, being careful of the medical line in the back of her hand. The breathing tube covers most of her face. The soft cushion patch of the strap stopping her skin from marking even more. The bruises look so dark against her unusually pale skin. The blood has been cleaned off, but she still doesn't look like my baby.

"Will she get better, Ace? Will she remember us? Oh God. He did a number on her."

"She'll remember us, Z. The connection is too strong for her to forget."

"Did you kill that twat?" she asks, anger lacing her voice. I shake my head, failure settling in again. I clench my fist, refusing to meet her disappointed eyes.

"You will. I believe in you and the club. Just make him hurt before you end him." My head snaps up at her words.

No other words are spoken between us for the rest of the night. I go out to tell the boys how she's doing and that they should go home, but they all refuse. Lola and the other old ladies come back with food for everyone. The club has taken over the waiting room, but not excluding other family members of other patients.

Solar pops in to see Ana before he sends a text to Jasmine to give her an update. Each of the boys come into the room one at a time to give Ana their love and wishes. This... this is why I fucking love my club; the Unforgiven Riders.

Zarah is sleeping in the chair in the corner, resting her head on her arm, looking uncomfortable. But she refused to go home. We've been here for seven days, and no changes from Ana. Well, they took her off the breathing machine and she has been coping great on her own, but the doc told us that with the brain injury, it may take a while for her to actually wake up.

I'm still holding Ana's hand, too scared to let go.

"I hope you can hear me, babe. I miss you. I need you to come back to us, to come back to me. I love you, Ana. I love you so fucking much. We are so fucking scared you won't remember us, but I have to believe our connection is strong enough for you to know everything about us." I kiss her hand and rest my head on the bed, falling into a nightmare.

I see the events of that night happening all over again, but this time Ana is screaming, telling me to protect our little girl crying in the corner. I'm torn about who to save, because we don't have a daughter. I run at the little girl when I hear a gunshot, and I turn just in time to see Ana falling to the floor.

"ANA!" I scream.

I startle awake, looking around the room, trying to focus. I look towards Ana and see that she's looking at me with a frown on her face.

My heart sinks.

Oh fuck, no...

She doesn't know who I am.

Ana

THE BEEPING OF A MACHINE WAKES ME UP. I BLINK A FEW TIMES, trying to clear the sleepy fog in my eyes. Where am I? My eyes clear and I look around the room. A hospital.

What happened?

Movement from my left startles me. I look down at the man lying there, clearly having a nightmare. In a flash, he's sitting upright, screaming my name.

"ANA!" I jump, then watch as he takes in the room before his gaze lands on me. He frowns and then smiles at me. It seems forced, but it's handsome.

"Ana, baby. You're awake. Oh, thank fuck." That voice sends shivers through my body. Why does his voice sound so familiar? We stare at each other like we're trying to communicate silently.

"Ana?" A voice I do know comes from behind the man. My sister, Zarah. "Oh God, you're awake. Ace, she's awake." I watch as he nods sadly. My eyes flicker between the two of them. Why does my heart hurt to see the sadness on his face? He steps back, letting my sister come closer.

"Ana?" My gaze snaps to hers, and I offer her a smile. I swallow, and it hurts. My hand goes to my throat. The man jumps and gets me a cup of water.

"I'll get the doc," he says sadly, and leaves the room. My eyes follow him out.

"Ana. Do you remember him." I shake my head. Her eyes fill with tears, and she cups my jaw. I wince, and she pulls her hands back. "That's Ace, Smallie. He's your boyfriend. You love him, and he loves you." My eyes shoot back to the door as the man walks back in, a doctor following close behind.

"Hello, Ana, my name is Doctor Sullivan, but you can call me Sully." I nod slowly. I sit there and answer the questions he asks. He checks my eyes and eye movement. I get a little annoyed at the light in my eyes, and I pull my head back.

My eyes find Ace again as he leans against the wall. He looks so sad. His gaze meets mine, and he smiles at me, his teeth breaking through his beard. The beard that feels amazing between my thighs. The beard that scratches my chin when he kisses me. I raise my hand to my mouth, and he licks his lips.

Wham!

Everything comes flooding back. A heart-breaking sob breaks free from my mouth. He's at my side in a second.

"Baby?"

"Ace. I remember you. Oh God, how could I forget?" I cry.

"Oh baby, it was going to take time. I would have been here no matter how long it took. God, I fucking love you, Ana." He kisses me gently, making sure not to hurt my face any more than it is. Now his eyes are beaming with happiness, which is far better than the sadness I saw just now.

"I'm here. What happened?" I cup his cheek, and wince when the IV pulls in my hand. "Tell me." I have no clue how I got here.

"What do you remember?" Sully asks. I close my eyes and the images flick through my brain.

"The cafe and the club, Nancy dying. Things start getting blurry after that." I gasp and look at Ace. He must see the hurt in my eyes as I remember him and Clover.

"Don't. That is done, and we moved past it," he admits. I look to Zarah, and she's nodding in agreement with Ace.

"Okay. I don't remember things after that, Doctor...?" I look at the doctor standing next to my bed.

"Sullivan, but you can call me Sully." Why does that sound familiar?

By the look on his face and Ace's, he has already told me that.

"You told me that just now, didn't you?" I bite my lip to keep the emotion under control.

"I did, Ana, but this is to be expected. Recovery for this type of injury has no limits. Things will get better in time; you just have to be patient. All of you." He turns and looks at Ace and Zarah.

"Got it. Not sure Ace knows what the word means." Zarah winks at me and Ace gives her the middle finger. I chuckle and then wince when my face hurts.

Sully explains my injuries, but thank God Ace will remember, because by the looks of it, I have some short-term memory loss. That will affect my day to day life, the cafe, my friends.

The doctor leaves and so does Zarah. She said she was going to fill in the club on what was happening, and then going home to rest up and shower.

"Can I have a mirror, please?"

"You don't need to see the damage, babe."

"Ace?" I plead. He nods and walks out of the room, only to return a few seconds later with a small compact mirror. I take a deep breath and gasp when the pain hits. I frown and look down.

"Broken ribs, baby," Ace tells me—again most probably. I nod. He holds the mirror in front of my face, and I gasp again. My face is black and blue with some purple and red patches.

Holy bloody hell.

They told me Gary and his men kidnapped and beat me, but no rape was performed, thank God. They did explain my injuries, but I can't seem to retain the information. I touch my face gingerly, careful not to add too much pressure on the bruises. I'm glad I can open my eyes because Ace told me one of them was swollen shut.

"Still beautiful, sweetheart," Ace tells me, kissing the side of my head.

I shake my head, causing the room to spin a little. Ace stops my head movement, cupping both my cheeks. "Always."

I suck in a breath at that word. That one word he always mutters to me. It's either 'always' or 'always last'. I touch my cheek, my cheekbone, my nose. I look like I went ten rounds with Anthony Joshua and lost miserably.

Tears fill my eyes. I don't bother stropping them; they need to fall. I need to let it all out and not let that sick man win. He will never control me again.

I am me; Ana Dawkins. The Sergeant-at-Arms of the Unforgiven Riders' old lady.

"Did you get him?" I ask Ace. He shakes his head.

"No, babe. He got away, but we are looking for him, so is Horton. We know Gary has connections, so his people may just hide him away for a while, but we will find the fucker." I give him a small smile. I believe every word he says. I know he will protect me no matter what, and so will the club.

I tap the bed next to me, indicating for Ace to join me. He doesn't waste any time climbing on and settling next to me. We snuggle in and watch football on the small TV on the wall. My body relaxes into his and I fall asleep, feeling safe and content.

Can anyone ever get irritated with being waited on hand and foot? I've been home from the hospital for two weeks, and I haven't been able to do anything for myself. I am not lying. If I need to pee, Ace is there to carry me to the bathroom. If I want a drink, Ace is there getting it for me.

Okay, so maybe I do need his help some of the time, like

when I forgot where the bathroom was at his place, or when I went to drink cranberry juice because it looked nice, but it turns out I don't like the stuff.

My temper flairs more than it did before. I called Zarah a bitch the other day because she stood a little close to Ace. I accused her of trying to steal him from me.

We said a few choice words and she walked out. Ace didn't talk to me for a few hours, but I refused to apologize. Then I took a nap and woke up and made them some dinner. They were giving me strange looks, like I had done something wrong. So I asked them.

"What? What's with the looks?" I ask them both.

"What do you mean, what? You called your sister a bitch earlier and accused her of trying to steal me from you. You were a bitch to her." My gaze bounces between them both, Zarah looking at me with sad eyes.

"What? Why would I do that? I know she would never do that to me." My nose starts to sting with tears. I take a deep breath, thanking God my ribs don't hurt so bad now.

"You tell me?" Ace mutters.

"Z?"

"I really hope you recover quickly, Ana. The way you were today... it really hurt my feelings."

"I'm sorry." I got up from the table and locked myself in my room. I cried myself to sleep, glad they let me be.

Which brings me to now, two days later. Ace brings in my drink and sets it on the coffee table. He sits next to me, carefully bringing me to his side, as we settle into watch more flipping TV. I need to get out of the house. I've been cooped up for long enough.

"I need to leave. I need to get out of here," I demand.

"You aren't ready to go anywhere yet," Ace mutters.

"Take me out," I demand again, knowing I'm acting like a brat. I climb to my feet. I place my good hand on my hip and look down at the man who has been keeping me locked away from the world.

Ace looks up at me and sighs. He rubs his hands over his face, looking more tired than normal. I know he misses going on runs for the club and being there.

"Let's go to the clubhouse. You can sit with the boys and I can sit with—" I frown because I can't think of her name. I can see her face in my head, but her name is escaping me. My fists clench and my heartrate picks up, frustration building inside me.

"FUCK," I growl. I never used to swear, but lately it's all I do. The doctors told us there would be some behavioural changes in me, and that my memory would come back. I was just happy that my injury hasn't affected my movement. Everything may go back to normal, but there's no time limit on a brain injury recovery.

"Baby, you know I love it when you say the word 'fuck'. Lola, babe, her name is Lola." He winks at me, but I scowl at him. I adjust the sling that's keeping my injured shoulder in place and walk out of the room. I walk up the stairs and into his room. How I plan to get dressed without him is beyond me, but I will try, even if it kills me.

"You need help, babe."

"Shut up." I use my free hand to pull open the drawer and yank out a pair of black leggings. Slamming that one shut, I open the next and pull out a t-shirt.

"Baby, stop." He sighs and moves me from the dresser. I watch as he moves to the wardrobe and pulls out my beige maxi dress that as a cute brown belt. I haven't been on the back of his bike since the before the incident, so I can wear this. He gets me dressed and helps me slip my feet into my sandals, all without words.

"Let's go," he mutters, and I follow him out to his car.

———

We drive to the clubhouse in complete silence. My palms are sweating, different things are running through my head as I try to figure out what is up with my man. He drives into the compound, nodding at Bear who opens the gate. Once he parks the car, he takes a deep breath and climbs out, before helping me out.

We walk into the clubhouse, Ace's hand resting on my hip. I gasp when I see what is in front of me. The clubhouse is filled with people. Members of the club, all the brothers, are looking clean cut and smiling at us. Zarah is standing next to Mae, smiling with tears in her eyes. Why is she crying? I look up and see the 'Glad you are feeling better' banner that's been painted in a sheet by the looks of things.

I walk over to my sister and hug her, before I turn to hug Mae. I don't call her by her club name because I can never remember it.

"Baby, come here." Ace calls me over to the bar. Zarah looks at me, her smile covering her beautiful face. I cup her cheek.

"Thank you for being you. My sister. My saviour." Tears flow down both our faces, but I leave her there and walk over to Ace by the bar. He hands me a cup of tea. I smile at him and lean in to kiss his cheek. Sitting on the stool, I add sugar to my tea, but see something is written on the spoon. The room goes dead silent. I look closer and gasp.

'Will you marry me?'

I turn my head to look at Ace but find him on his knee next to me. I cover my hand over my mouth and cry at the sight of this beautiful man on knees before me.

"Ana, my baby. I kneel before you, as you have knelt before me in the past." He winks at me when I gasp and blush to high heaven.

"I love you more than life itself. I have promised to protect you, and I have failed, but no more. I will protect you with my life. You will have my heart, my soul, and my body whenever the fuck you want it." He spreads his arms out wide, making the room burst into cat calls. "I chased you until you caved, and I am so fucking happy you did. We have had such a journey to get here, but we did it. I have you as my old lady, but I want my ring on your finger, and one day my baby in your belly. Will you marry me and be mine? Always!"

I gasp when he opens the small black box and I see the ring inside. It is a round opal stone, set in a white gold band that has diamonds framing it. It's perfect.

"Answer the poor man," someone calls out, and the room laughs with him. I smile down at Ace and nod.

"Always, Ace. Always."

He leaps to his feet and kisses me like a starving man. The room erupts into cheers for us, but I fade them out and give my soon-to-be husband my full attention. But that doesn't last long, as we are pulled apart and congratulated by everyone in the room. I'm hugged and kissed on the cheek more times that I can count.

I lean against the bar and watch as the room celebrates our engagement. Ace saddles up to me, tucking me into his side and leaning in and kissing my cheek.

"One more thing," Ace says, pointing to the box Lola just set on the bar top. I frown and pull off the lid. I move the navy paper and gasp.

There lies my leather cut. The club's logo stares back at me, but it's the words that catch my attention.

Property of Ace.

"Always last."

He kisses my lips and cups my bum in his big hand.

"Definitely always last."

Ace McGowan will always be my forever and always.

Ana

WELL, TODAY IS MY WEDDING DAY. WHO WOULD HAVE THOUGHT I would get married again? Today is a day for happiness, no sadness or negatively allowed.

I stand in front of the long mirror in Ace's room at the club-house and take in my dress that Lola had made for me. Look at me remembering her name. My memory and my behavior have got so much better over the last four months.

My dress is white with a free-flowing skirt with sections that are lace and silk. The deep-ish v-neck is held together by a thin layer of lace. Lace also covers the tops of my shoulders, and there's a thick lace band around my waist. I lay my hand over my flat stomach and smile at the secret I'm keeping.

I've kept my hair down with a slight wave to it. I'm not into fussy things at all. My first wedding for a full frilly thing and I hated it.

My bridesmaids are in simple sage green, strapless maxi dresses, with their hair up in a messy bun and a small flower arrangement.

"You are beautiful, Smallie," Zarah chokes out from behind me. It's been an emotional day. I turn to look at my sister and smile through the tears. She is absolutely stunning.

"So are you, sweets. Oh God." I batter my eyelashes and fan my face to stop the tears.

"NO! No crying today, bitches," Mae states while walking into the room, looking as pretty as ever in her bridesmaid dress. Zarah looks at me and winks, before walking over to pick up my bouquet. It's perfect for me. It's made of wild feathers with different wooden pine cones and flowers and some thin twigs. The colours are amazing.

"No crying," we state.

"Nope, unless you're crying out from the biker orgasm you'll be getting later tonight—or knowing Ace, in an hour." Mae winks at me and I laugh.

"True. I can't wait to see him in his tux. I was very surprised he agreed with me on that."

"Smallie, Ace would give you the world if he could."

"And a thousand orgasms?" Mae adds.

"Girl, what is with you and orgasms lately?" Zarah asks her.

Mae sighs. "EC is killing me. He started turning up at the cafe when I'm working. Texting me."

"And the problem with that is?" I prompt.

"There are two problems with that. One: he really hurt me. Two: Levi." Mae looks miserable. I walk over and kneel in front of her to hug her. Being torn between two men is something I have never had to deal with, so I can't imagine what she's thinking.

"Woman, take them both to bed. I will say this, EC is not the man he was when we first arrived. He's grown up. The club girls have been bitching because he isn't touching them," Zarah tells her, and I nod. I've heard the girls saying bad things about him. You can never please these bitches.

"Talk to him. Talk to them both. If I have learned anything in the last few years, it's that nothing will happen unless you make it happen. I could have died when Gary took me, but I held onto the hope that Ace and the club would save me, and they did. If you want both of them, then you'll find a way to make it work."

A knock on the door pulls us from our girl time.

"Are you decent in here?" Suede's voice comes through the door.

"Come on in, old man," Zarah calls out, smirking at us girls.

"I'll give you old man. I can put you over my knee, little girl." He grins when he warns her.

"Oh, I don't doubt it. But I think your old lady would have a thing or two to say about that," Zarah muses back.

"Fuck yeah, she would." He winks at her and then turns to me. His smile goes from amused to serious in a heartbeat. "Oh, bloody hell, Ana. You are fucking beautiful, darlin'. Your parents would be so damned proud of you. Of both of you. They are up there." He points to the sky, and tears start to appear again. Mae will go nuts if I cry. I look over at her and my sister, and they are both crying. I cough out a laugh.

"No crying you said." Mae waves me off and wipes her eyes.

"They are looking down on today and they are smiling at you both, thanking the fucking Lord Jesus Christ that you are both happy and well. So is our Nancy. So how about we let them watch you get married today to my boy, yeah?" I nod, taking note of my heartbeat beating a mile a minute.

"See you out there," Zarah says, and the girls exit the room.

"Let's do this," Suede says. It was an emotional day when Suede asked if he could walk me down the aisle to Ace. Even Ace had a tear or two in his eyes.

We walk out the door and over to where the ceremony is being held at the back of the club's property. Lola thought the space could be used for other weddings, so she had the boys flatten the land and resurface the grass. I let Lola and Zarah do the decorating. I just told them what I wanted.

I gasp when I see the ceremony area. There are mason jars everywhere filled with candles; on the surfaces, hanging from branches. There are also bottles filled with wildflowers. Everyone is sitting on white chairs with a sage green sash wrapped around and tied in the back. I see the brothers from the club all wearing their club cuts over a white shirt and tie, with black trousers. They look so handsome.

It's the little things you notice on a day like today. I spot little packets of bird seed, that also says confetti on there. Might as well feed the birds while we're at it. I see the smiling faces of people that I know, and some that I don't. I know we have other chapters here today, and some members from another club.

I turn my head to the front and gasp when I see Ace standing there. I stop in my tracks and try to catch my breath. He looks so handsome in a full tux. His hair is combed back perfectly, and he trimmed his beard. My man looking fine in all his glory.

We move again and I'm taken to the man I'm about to marry and spend the rest of my life with.

"She is all yours, brother," Suede says when we reach the altar. Ace gives him a nod and takes my hands. We face each other, and Ace moves in to kiss me. The priest coughs and people laugh at him.

"Not yet," he whispers, winking.

"Fucking beautiful, baby."

"Handsome, honey."

"Let's begin. We are gathered here today to watch this man, take this woman as his old lady and wife. We aren't going to do the usual spiel we would do in church, because let's to be honest, Ace does not have the patience for that." Everyone laughs and shouts out their agreement. "I do believe these two have written their own vows. Ace," the priest prompts.

"Ana, you are my world, plain and simple. My heart beats for you. My engine revs for you." He winks at me and I shake my head, smiling. "I will *always* love and protect you. I will *always* be by your side, supporting you in everything you do. I love you, baby. *Always.*"

"Short and sweet. I like it. Ana," the priest says.

"Ace, you will always own my heart and the air in my lungs— which you steal regularly with your handsomeness." I wink at him. "I will *always* love and protect you. I will *always* be at your side, supporting you in everything you do. I love you, honey. *Always*."

"Be safe. Be kind. Be loyal. I now pronounce you man and wife. You may *now* kiss your beautiful bride." Ace doesn't waste a second before he pounces on me, taking a kiss so strong he brands me with his lips and his love, just like the brand on my right wrist.

I break the kiss and look deep into his eyes. The love that shines from him is overwhelming, and my eyes fill with tears.

"Ace, I have something to tell you." Nerves bundle in my belly. I take his hands and lay them on my stomach. I hear gasps from beside us, but I don't take my eyes off my husband. His eyes drop, then snap back up to mine.

"You serious?" I nod, biting my lip to keep my emotions under control.

"You're fucking pregnant? You're going to have my baby?" I nod again. He picks me up and spins me around, making me giggle.

"We're having a baby," he yells to all the wedding guests. Cheers and clapping fill the air around us, making this the best day ever.

Today I got to become Mrs. McGowan. Today I got to share with my new husband that we are expanding the McGowan family. Suede was right: both my parents and Nancy are looking down on us, proud as chips we're giving them a grandchild.

Arms wrap around me from behind, resting on my stomach as I smile and watch our guests partying like they haven't before.

"I fucking love you, Mrs. McGowan."

"I fucking love you, too, Mr. McGowan.

"Forever and always, baby."

"Always last," I say as he kisses me on the cheek.

Always is a very long time, but a time that will flourish and will cherish.

Epilogue
Part 2

Ace

This is the life I never thought I wanted, but here I am, sitting here with a beauty in my arms. Her head resting on my chest as I watch her body rise and fall with each delicate breath she takes. I gently run my hand over her head, careful not to wake her up.

She loves her sleep but is easily woken. She was like a whirlwind when she came into my life, completely taking over my cold heart. The way she makes me feel... she gives me the need to be a better man. Her lips pucker, and it brings a smile to my face.

The stairs creak behind me, but I don't turn around. I know who it is. The other woman in my life.

"Honey, she's asleep; you can put her down now," Ana says as she sits on the couch next to me. I smile at her, leaning in for a kiss. She meets me halfway.

"I know I can, baby. I just don't want to. I like holding her. This is daddy-daughter time. The brothers never let me hold her when they're here or we're at the clubhouse." I pout. Ana laughs softly, looking at our baby girl in my arms.

"She does have them wrapped around her little fingers." I gently pick up her hand, toying with her tiny fingers against my large hands.

"My Blaire will have all the brothers running around after her one day, I can tell you now. They will chase and protect her against the world."

I'm right, because that's what the Unforgiven Riders are all about.

Family.

Love.

Loyalty.

Brotherhood.

The End

ACKNOWLEDGMENTS

My baby, my boss man. Thank you for standing beside me and helping me overcome huge arse hurdles.

My 3 babies. Always remember I love you and I'm so proud of you.

My #bookbestie Kelly, thank you for always telling me I 'can do it' and for pushing me to write an MC series. #AceIsClaimed

Thank you Dana Leah, yet again you blow the cover design out of the water!

And Stephanie Farrant.... thank you for sticking with me and for making Claiming Mime readable.

Krissy V & Sienna Grant, thank you for helping with the blurb. They are the Devils Bitch

Sammy, my #HeadBitch thank you for the support you have given me.

My betas, Kara, Tracy, Mandi and Kathleen thank you for all the help with this book. You are rockstars.

And to my readers. A HUGE thank you for standing by me and supporting me. Thank you for falling in love with my characters.

ABOUT THE AUTHOR

Author Bio

Hey, I'm Amy. I'm married to an amazing man, and we have 3 amazing kids. I'm from South Wales, UK. I fell in love with writing when I was at school (many moons ago) but it never fully bloomed until later in life. Music plays a big part in my life, so does photography.

I write contemporary romance and I also enjoy reading it. I'm a big fan of MC and mafia bools. I have this weird thing when writing my books, I love to put friends and family names into my books. So look out for that

I enjoy knowing my books help readers escape their day to day life, like most author do with me!

Always remember, never forget!

More books by Amy Davies

Let Me Love You
Rafe (The Phoenix Boys Series book 1)
Ryder (The Phoenix Boys Series book 2)
Reeve (The Phoenix Boys Series book 3)
What Are The Chances
This Time Around
Dex (Castle Ink book 1)
Jay (Castle Ink book 2)

Ivy (Castle Ink book 3)
Defeating the Odds
Christmas at Paradise Meadows

37551785R00110

Made in the USA
Middletown, DE
28 February 2019